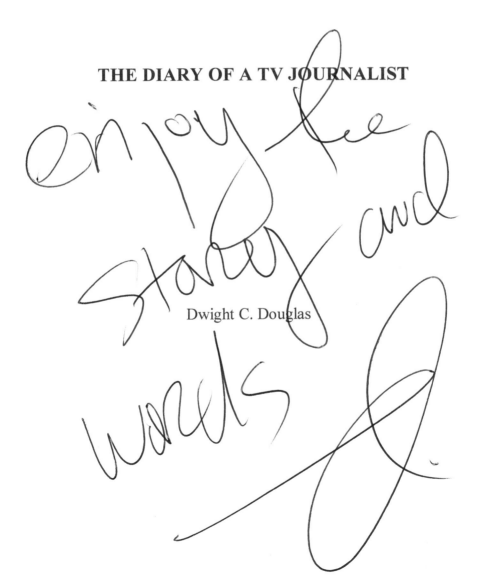

If God Could Talk...

THE DIARY OF A TV JOURNALIST

Dwight C. Douglas

DEDICATION

For my wonderful children: Courtney, Taylor, Amanda and Danielle.
May you find God, or someone like her, to give you the strength and
confidence to find happiness in this world.

Table of Contents

1. Beginning

Do you believe in God? It's a pretty simple question. If you answer the question without thinking, then you may never have had a reason to doubt your belief in a deity. But perhaps, you aren't quite sure and that uncertainly could be based on what you've been taught or in questioning what you've been taught. Ah, that great magnifying-glass, logic. What do you truly believe? We aren't talking about that euphemism that some people toss around - "belief system." For one thing, why would the word "system" ever be near the word "belief"? A belief isn't a mechanical or worldly concept or even a logical process. It should be a deep-seeded, faith-based conviction, arrived at by instruction, experience, observation or some combination of the three. It doesn't follow the same pattern of development in everyone. Do you live by some lasting life principle?

This is not about how you answer your mother-in-law or even your shrink. Do you possess some kind of morality-driven sense of common humanism or do you carry with you a fear-driven mandated morality that was stamped on your forehead by your parents or some religious authority? My desire is not to pass judgment on what you reckon to be right, but to tell my story.

I didn't know why, but during this period I kept having the same dream: There I was sitting on a stone bench in the middle of a graveyard. While the wind blew the dust into swirling circles, I heard my mother's voice. She wasn't far off in the distance. Through the whistling wind I heard her urging, "Jonas, don't get your nice suit dirty, we're about to leave for church." The wind picked up… and then, I woke up.

As light came to the surface, the sound of one-thousand crows was outside my window; so dense a murder the early spring trees appeared to have a full head of leaves. Large black leaves. If I were a superstitious man, I would have assumed that something ominous was about to happen. If I were an overly religious man, I would have been thumbing through my King James Version attempting to find some greater meaning. But in fact, this day would turn out to be the beginning of a most amazing journey.

It had been one thousand days since I came to New York to begin one of the best jobs of my career. In the short span of nearly three years I had taken a prime-time talk show on a sinking cable channel and breathed life into the old battleship. Along with the ratings I had been rewarded with tons of publicity because of my interviews with kings, captives and movie stars. But something was missing. I was still in search of that one interview that would put me over the top and guarantee my place in the history of television, like Edward R. Murrow, David Frost, or Mike Wallace.

I got out of bed and began my daily routine. First, a fistful of colorful vitamins and nutrients washed down with a large gulp of orange juice were part of the rite. As I stared down at the Central Park West traffic from my penthouse co-op, I imagined the tiny yellow and green cabs were pills in the blood stream of morning traffic. I took another swig of juice and noticed the label on the plastic bottle that assured me that I was getting "medium pulp." I wondered why people buy O.J. without pulp. Why would you consume something so natural but demand that the juice company take the best part out? Then I chuckled. Why did I buy the one with medium pulp? Perhaps this was my character-flaw, wanting to know as much as possible about how things work and what people thought, but never becoming emotionally committed. This was my medium pulp life, lots of friends but no one person in my life.

My name is Jonas Bronck; named after the seventeen-century Dutch immigrant who settled in what is now the greater New York City area. In fact, the Bronx River (Bronck's River) and the borough of the city of New York were named after the original Jonas Bronck. The name has been both a gift and a burden for me. No one seems to be able to spell it but once they get it, they remember it. Even that first TV job exploited it by naming the consumer show: "The Bronck Busters" where I headed up a team of consumer fraud reporters; a "Ghostbuster"-type of late '80s reporters saving Pittsburgh from the bad guys.

With my life taking me through several local TV stations and a few unsuccessful attempts at publishing some books, I felt it fitting that Jonas Bronck's namesake had returned to New York and, for the most part, become successful. But how do we judge success? What is really important in life? There never seems to be time to ponder such weighty matters. The clock is ticking; it's time to get to work.

The great thing about being a big personality on a major cable network is that all your on-camera clothing is provided by the company. The wardrobe room for the show was a wonderful collection of top-quality threads to don before I walked in front of the bright lights. Getting dressed to make the short, seven block trip to the office was no big chore. I threw on a shirt, pair of jeans and a comfortable old jacket. The producers of the show called it my "professor look." The jackets were sans leather elbow-patches, of course. We were in New York.

I rarely shaved in the morning, always left that task for late in the afternoon so that my face, with its deftly applied TV makeup, would appear smooth as a baby's butt. Not that a 50-year-old man really ever looks like a young set of cells. I really never enjoyed the show biz part of being on TV. I was trained to be a journalist and writer. I truly believed the Fourth Estate had some responsibility to uncover scams, reveal truths and help the unwashed understand what is really happening in the world. My idealism, however, never got in the way of negotiating a better deal with each step I climbed on the broadcasting ladder.

One of the professional perks of a great broadcasting job was a car that picked you up and took you home. I declined that convenience and always opted for taking a taxi. It seemed more exciting to get into a cab in New York and feel at one with the flow and energy of this great city. Having the sunrise on the back of my neck as we wove and worked our way through the morning traffic helped me to wake up.

From the moment each day started, I would read my email, check all the news sites and send my producer ideas for the next interview. My tablet never left my side. In fact, I had a few pockets increased in size so I could have the world at my fingertips. The tablet became more like a companion than a device.

As I pulled up to the News Center building I paid the cabbie. He looked at me as he gave me my change and receipt, he asked, "Hey, aren't you…"

I smiled and slid out to the curb, "Yes, that's me."

I scanned left to right and moved toward the front door. The morning sun reflected off the corporate logo emblazed on the marble frames of the front door, another reminder that I was doing serious work here. Maybe there was a little bit of pride and the need to be recognized that propelled me, that tiny bit of an ego boost to get me started, like a jolt of black coffee. I was excited about being in the most important city in the world with a powerful platform of expression. Deep down inside I kept hearing that little voice say, "You made it. You really made it."

No matter how big and successful you are there is usually another force at work. Your significance is fleeting and no matter how great you think you are, you have to remember you have a boss. It's like that old expression, "Everyone has a boss except God and he has a fierce competitor."

I wasn't thinking about competitors or bosses that day. I was just happy to be alive. But I was about to find out that this was no normal day. This moment would be etched into my mind like a bad dream played over and over in a movie that never seemed to end. I thought that writing this all out would help me make the memory loop stop. It helped in a cathartic way, but nothing seems to erase the memory of what was about to follow.

As unbelievable as it may seem, this story changed my life forever. You just need to believe and this will all make sense. I think they call it, faith.

2.   Mysterious Lunch

We all have routines when we arrive at our workplace, those things we do to feel more in sync with the ever-turning gears of an organization. As I walked through the lobby I looked up at the giant statue of the naked man. My eyes gravitated toward his bronze male organ, polished to a light shade of cream by tourists who used it as a backdrop for their souvenir photos. I always wondered why they just didn't leave artwork well enough alone.

I stopped at the gift shop at the base of the escalators and picked up a paper. I had already consumed most of the stories online but, there was something about having a real newspaper in my hand as I walked through those massive doors with the TNN logo emblazoned on the glass that made the news seem more important. If you're in the right position, the well-lit logo behind the reception desk lines up to the logo on the door. That kind of symmetry had always intrigued me; someone planned this "coincidence." I smiled and offered a good morning to the receptionist. She smiled and nodded.

Moving down the hall I saw people on phones and screens scanning for the latest weather charts, the competitors' breaking news and social network updates.

We seemed so connected, yet hardly connected to each other. As I got to the end of the hall and unlocked the door to my corner office overlooking Columbus Circle, I hesitated and took a deep breath. It was a new week; it was a Monday.

I wasn't in my office for more than 12 seconds before my executive producer Gloria Madoffa was in my face. "Good morning Jonas, what do you need for the meeting?"

Not looking up, I answered, "Good morning to you, too. Just bring the schedule and folder. Give me 20 minutes to clear some mail."

Gloria turned in one motion, "Roger that."

That's the thing about young people today. They are either so repulsively self-absorbed, or totally obsessed with success. Of course, I've always surrounded myself with "type-As" who understand how to use language and question everything, so I shouldn't find abrupt behavior surprising, I guess.

One of the devices I found harder and harder to use was the desk telephone. I was reshaped by the Internet just like most people. I found myself sending an email to someone across the office rather than going to talk to them face to face. It just seemed so much more efficient, but I did feel like we were all moving apart like the ever-expanding universe. The industry seemed more interested in "trending" than defending the First Amendment. Media was more focused on famously faux personalities than real newsmakers. We spend hours looking at little screens, medium screens and larger screens. I snapped back to reality when I realized that if people stopped looking at those screens, I would be out of a job.

As I clicked through my phone messages on the voice-mail system, I deleted calls that had already been answered and pitches from Wall Street brokers trying to get my money, but I stopped on one blinking message. It was from someone who had been very helpful to me since I arrived in New York: Ida Pearlstein, one of the best booking agents in the business. She rarely called on a Monday but judging by the time of the call — 6:45 a.m. — I knew something was up.

I played the message, "Jonas B, this is Ida P, I **must** have lunch with you today, darling. Please cancel whatever you have. This is the guest of a lifetime. Call me as soon as you get this."

I erased the message, called Gloria, and asked her to come to my office. She appeared in seconds, "Yeah, what's up?"

I paused, and then asked, "Gloria, do you know why Ida Pearlstein would want to have lunch?" I looked out at the traffic going counter-clockwise around the circle. Behind my back I heard the clicking of her iPhone keyboard.

"Nope. She didn't send me an email," She answered.

I scratched my head, "Something is going on. Who could the interview be with? I hope this isn't one of those studios demanding that we put some half-baked actor on the air just to boost attendance at the opening weekend of a movie. That will piss me off."

As she left the office Gloria added, "Why don't you call her, already?"

So I did, and as soon as Ida said hello I could hear that something was wrong. Her voice seemed frantic and stressed. I asked her if everything was alright and she said, "Yes, but I don't have much time. I will explain at lunch."

We picked an old Indian restaurant on Central Park South. The owner and I had grown close over the years and he understood my desire to be positioned with my back to the door in the alcove in the back. It was a dandy place to get some great food without the distraction of people coming up to the table.

When I got there Rajiv said Mrs. Pearlstein had already been seated. I got to the table and looked into her eyes as I gave her a handshake and a peck on the cheek. Her perfume cut through the curry and after exchanging pleasantries, she got to the point.

"I have a guest that'll put you on the front page of every newspaper in the world."

I laughed, "Okay, Ida, it's not April Fools' Day — or is this where I get to actually kill a guest while I'm interviewing him?"

She barely laughed, "Jonas, I'm serious. You have to suspend disbelief for a second and listen to me."

With a more serious tone, I said, "Ida, I'm all ears. What's this all about?"

It was as if the air was sucked out of the room. The audio dropped out. No one was moving. The woman in her late 60s bit her lip, then turned to me, "This Wednesday, two days from now, I will be eating lunch. In the middle of the lunch, I will have a massive heart attack and die."

Now I was worried. I had experienced something like this in my mother when her mental awareness slowly fell away and she slipped into the grip of Alzheimer's. I took a sip of water, and carefully formulated my words, gently guarding my facial expressions, "What do you mean by this, Ida?"

"I know you think I am crazy. You should. I think it's totally nuts," She continued.

I looked up at her, "So, you're just messing with me, right?"

"Jonas, I've had a great run. It's going to happen to all of us one day," She broke a smile

I took a deep breath and got a bit more forceful, "Why would you say this?"

She leaned forward and lowered her voice, "He told me."

"Who would tell you such a terrible thing?" I demanded.

She laughed, "The person I want you to interview. The reason I called you. The biggest show you'll ever do."

3.   The Reveal

The words of my favorite college English professor Claude Van Allen came to mind: "Always keep an open mind and see the many possible levels of every story. Light goes into a prism as white light but comes out the other side as a rainbow of possibilities." I looked down at the Chicken Tikka and then at this seasoned professional. I thought she had lost her marbles.

What I was about to hear was more fantastic and unbelievable than anything I could have imagined. I put my fork down and asked again, "Who might this person be?"

She smiled, leaned in and whispered as if to tell me a secret, "It's God."

I did everything I could not to laugh or cry; I wasn't sure. I rubbed my chin as if to ponder the proposal.

She had a look of intensity, "Jonas, do have any idea what this means?"

With a more intense voice I answered, "You know, Ida, this seems like a trick. I know, you have always delivered for me — but this feels like some kind of setup."

She closed her eyes, and went into a trance, "You will know the truth and he will be delivered unto you in time," She recited as if conveying a word-for-word message.

Now I was spooked. Was she acting out some kind of hallucination to make me think some power had taken over her thoughts? The malady had gotten hold of her mind.

"Ida, let's back up. Let me see if I get this. You have a way to give me God, not sure which one, but he or she — or it — will agree to go on TV live and talk to me? Really?"

She opened her eyes and grinned, "Yes, I knew you would get it. I know that's why he picked you. You'll ask the right questions."

I shook my head in a patronizing way, "Well, that is something; God picked Jonas Bronck to interview him. And when will this interview take place?"

She smiled a bigger smile, "Well, it will be after I am gone. He will contact you. You'll know. That's all I know. My job was just to facilitate." She got serious again "The only thing I ask, my dear Jonas, is that when the press pressures you into disclosing how this happened, that you make it clear that I helped you get this interview; that's all I request."

Answering quickly and in the most convincing way I could, I said, "Of course, this is the Pearlstein touch. You should get all the credit. I'm just the funny guy on TV getting a chance to interview the most powerful force in the universe. That would make a good promo."

Ida clapped in joy, "Yes, now you're talking. You got it."

As I walked around Columbus Circle, I saw all the lonely gray faces in the cabs as they went round and round. I tried to shake what had just happened out of my brain. Was I drugged, or was she suffering from a fast onset of mental illness? She seemed lucid and in control of her faculties and she was convincing. But like most born-again souls, the path from light believer to obsessive zealot can be a short trip. At least she didn't suggest that it was Jesus. That would have been extremely ironic coming from one of the Jewish faith. I laughed and shook my head.

I got back into my office and prepared my notes for the 3 o'clock show formatting meeting. We usually did five segments of 34 minutes each. The flow of the show worked like this: every fifteen minutes we placed questions to create a strong tease right before the commercial break. For example, "Coming up, we'll ask Charlie Sheen what his relationship with his father is really like." The better the tease, the more likely the audience would stay with the channel during the ads.

Gloria was first in my office for the meeting, "So, how was your lunch with Ida? Who does she have for us?"

This is what I've always loved about Gloria, no-B.S., a real New Yorker. She wasted little time on small talk and got answers from people quickly. Growing up in Westchester County, she should have been a doctor or lawyer or a physicist like Mommy and Daddy, but she loved to chase fire trucks and police cars from an early age. Her deep auburn hair was usually free-form lioness and her slight New York accent gave her an in-your-face feeling. But her intellect made you grasp her depth as soon as you met her. Her expressive thick lower-lip, rarely used to pout, could spout truck driver raw as well as Shakespearean rhyme. Gloria used her penetrating brown-eyed stare to bring the most hardened liar to the truth.

She wrote for her high school paper and caught the interest of a famous writer who lived in Scarsdale. He reinforced the possibilities of a writing career. After working as an intern at ABC network, while in school at Columbia, she fine-tuned her aggressive interviewing technique and managed to land a producer's job at the highest-rated investigative TV show. We were lucky to get her. As my executive producer, she brought a ton of trust to the team. She and I had no secrets.

I smiled and asked her over to the conference table. She sat down with a look of total concentration. She locked onto my next words.

"I have some bad news. I think Ida is suffering from some kind of breakdown, or maybe some kind of psychotic episode."

Gloria laughed out loud, and managed her quip, "Okay, we know that. All the booking agents are crazy. What did she want?"

"Before the others get here, let's agree to keep this one between you and me," I suggested

She nodded and put her pen in her mouth.

I continued, "She claims to have a guest for us, on an exclusive basis, of course." I paused, not believing that I'd said that, giving more credence to this ludicrous proposition. "She must have some early onset of Alzheimer's, or something; she claims to have God for us."

At this point Gloria, displaying her quick wit and sense of humor said "Okay, I think he would go great on a Thursday, last segment. Do you think he'll want more than the 34 minutes? I'm sure he'll have some other shows to do. Jon Stewart would love to get him!"

Now I was laughing at this sarcasm. "Okay but there is something quite disturbing in this whole thing; she says there will be a sign."

"Sure, there is always a sign but I don't think security will let us do the burning bush in the building," Gloria added.

I got serious, "No, apparently the rush for the lunch appointment was based on some inside information she received from God."

Gloria leaned forward, "Pray tell; what is the big…" she made air quotes with her hands, *message from God.*"

I dropped the bomb, "Ida will have a massive heart attack at lunch on Wednesday and drop dead."

Gloria dropped her smile, "That's freakin' creepy."

4.   The Comprehension

Our guest that Monday night was an expert in airplane design, a sharp, well-known avionics inventor who suggested that we're rather Neanderthal in the way we handle our multi-million dollar flying machines. He pointed out that we spend hundreds of dollars on LoJack devices and security systems for our cars and homes but we have to call out the Marines to find a plane that falls into the ocean. Haven't we discovered another way to track things beyond satellites and radar? Imagine if someone could see everything that happened?

During that late afternoon planning meeting, the thought of Ida's lunchtime prediction kept barging into my mind. It disturbed me enough to pick up the phone and book an early morning session Tuesday with my shrink. Not that I'm crazy or anything.

I grew up as the youngest of four boys in Fort Wayne, Indiana. My father's history included years in the military and so most of my formative years were spent in a virtual boot camp. My older brothers had lower expectations than I did and two of them were happy to build RVs in Elkhart, Indiana. My brother Larry always wanted to be a soldier. He was a brave man but the first

Gulf War ended his military career and his life. That is when I started to see a professional.

When I moved to New York, a friend of mine made a joke about how her psychiatrist had a wicked sense of humor. I quipped, "Sure would like to pay someone to sit there and laugh at my stories." That's how I got Dr. Theodore Brickman's number and signed up for what I called "occasional rebooting." Ted was a good listener. Of course, most good doctors in that field have to be good listeners.

I've always believed that the indication that something has had major impact on your life is when it's the first thing that comes to mind when you wake up. The first thought that surfaced on this day was the offer from Ida Pearlstein and how I felt guilty about it. Why? Obviously this woman had some major malady. So why was I going to the shrink at 8 a.m. today? I got through my routine and jumped in a cab to the East Side.

Brickman, like many doctors in New York, worked out of a first floor apartment. His office was on Park Avenue. Yes, he was expensive, and even with our wonderful health insurance coverage I had to pay for most of what he charged. This would be only my second visit that year. I was his first patient that day, so his office door was open.

He greeted me with a large smile, "Come in, come in. What took you so long?"

I laughed and said, "Well, you are such a great doctor, I really need only a few visits."

He looked at me over his blue-framed reading glasses, "You know flattery will get you quite far with me." He laughed and offered me some coffee.

We sat down and after about 15 minutes of talking about stupid things like the weather and the government surveillance program, he zeroed in on me, "Jonas, I am sure you aren't here to discuss the NSA, what gives?"

I filled him in on what had happened the day before. He listened intently. Then, he took his glasses off and sighed, "I know Mrs. Pearlstein. We go to the same Temple. I don't think she has any obvious mental or health problems."

This became a bit uncomfortable because I wasn't here for an evaluation of what was going on with Ida. I was sitting there wanting to know why I had anxious feelings about what she said. I redirected the conversation back to me.

"Look Doc, I just feel like I should be doing something," I opened my arms, "I mean, if for some reason that woman dies tomorrow, I am going to have major guilt that I didn't do something."

Brickman opened his mouth almost as if the words were being processed while his face was in a freeze-frame. Finally, he spoke. "Jonas, tateleh, she's not going to die tomorrow. I'm sure she has no way to deliver God to you for an interview. Knowing their family, I'm sure God wouldn't even take her call."

I laughed, and we talked about my lack of meaningful connection with anyone from the opposite sex since I moved to New York. I repeated my standard response about being so busy and totally focused on my work. He nodded in the same way he'd responded the last three years. He gave me a prescription for something to help me with the lack of dopamine in my frontal lobes and I turned to leave.

In a TV detective, Columbo-like move, I turned back to ask one more question, "Say Doc, as I pointed to the empty chair, "If God was sitting in that chair what would ask him?"

On the quick, he said, "I'd say, can't you pick someone else?" I barely laughed.

He forced a laugh, and then I said, "What do you mean?"

His 79-year old face morphed into a serious position, "I sure know I don't want to die. You get to meet God after you die, right? I mean if there is a God. That's what I would say."

I scratched my chin, "So, the only time we see God is when he comes to take us? When we're ready to die?" I could see in his eyes that he was considering the time left for him was so much shorter than the time left for me.

There was a bit of what we call in the business 'dead air' and then Dr. Brickman added, "Well, you're a smart man and I ain't no spring chicken, but I am sure neither of us has ever seen God. Do you really think you are going to get him on TV? Now that *is* faith."

In a moment of extremely dark humor, I said, "Well, Ida has to drop dead first. After all, we have to keep this linear, right Doc?"

Brickman shook his head and waved, "Call me if you need me."

5.   The Fortune Teller

Tuesday night's show was not that memorable except for my last segment. I didn't really think the idea would work, but Gloria insisted that it might be unique. Who am I, a mere mortal, to argue with my executive producer? She had proven herself quite commendable over the years, with a shelf of Emmy awards to show for it. Intellectually we were so in sync that an outsider would think that there was more than a professional relationship going on there. It was not that we would finish each other's sentences, but we could clearly finish each other's thoughts.

One of the guests was a woman who had gained a lot of notoriety for a book she wrote about her experiences as a psychic. The other guest was a psychologist from Columbia University. The psychologist was Dr. Peter Draper and the clairvoyant was Estela Montague. One of the things about being on TV five nights a week is you must do your research, which means reading tons of pages from the guest's book and doing more than reading what Wikipedia has to say about them. We also have a team of researchers and interns we depended on to deliver on a ritual we call "vetting." It's what political candidates are supposed to do when they pick a running mate. The task of finding out things like: is the daughter of the running mate pregnant out of wedlock.

Draper was easy. I had interviewed him several times before and also had some social interaction with him at dinner functions. Estela was a blank slate to me but I am sure she knew everything about me. After all, she was a psychic.

During the vetting process, one of my researchers pointed out that 10 years ago, Montague had been very helpful in locating a small plane in a lake and a 1000-year-old-garment in a cave in Tibet. And 20 years ago she had predicted that we would have a black president in the United States. There were also her missed predictions, such as the Earth would be hit by an asteroid in 2000, or that Donald Trump would become president and that Jesus would come back to Earth on 12-12-12.

The researcher warned me that if the soothsayer felt Draper and I were ganging up on her, she would say outrageous things. I pondered if that was what I wanted out of her. It would make for better ratings. I always aimed for audience reaction.

The show started out in a quirky manner. Draper, who always took the position that this power of the mind over matter, extrasensory perception (ESP) and Psychokinesis (PK) was all just mumbo-jumbo, seemed to be veering from his science. On this night, he took a rapid turn toward the psychic Montague's point of view.

In most cases, our goal was to have guests with differing opinions so I could be the traffic cop. But that night I felt this need to push them both toward some kind of realism. What one of my researchers had failed to pick up on, of all things, was Dr. Draper's Facebook page. He had recently met a woman from India who was into all kinds of spiritual pillars, such as reincarnation and, of course, the general belief in mind over matter. It would have been as easy as finding out what the check box of "in a relationship" meant to Draper, a twice-divorced Columbia faculty member.

As the interview wore on, I kept the heat on both of them to prove that predicting the future, finding lost people or directly communicating with dead relatives was not even possible, much less provable. During the break, I heard Gloria's voice in my ear plug, "You seem rather on edge. Just back off a bit and let them tell some stories. It's just TV, Jonas."

Gloria is a smart broadcaster, an excellent reader of what the public wants. She also knew me like a book. I may have been coating my questions with a little bit of frustration. I kept thinking these people are convincing the audience that hallucinations and voices from dark places are real.

After we returned from the break, I lightened up a bit and listened as Draper added some rich cultural stories about people in India who have been able to talk to people in other worlds.

Dr. Draper was very convincing with, "Through prayer and meditation they have the ability to clear their minds of all thoughts so that the voices of the past can surface and be heard."

Estela Montague was able to relate some recent stories about finding a kidnapping victim, "A mother, whose daughter was kidnapped, believed that her daughter appeared in a dark room one night. A strange glow filled the room and she was able to hear her daughter's voice."

I sat forward, "What did she say?"

She pushed her hair back, "The daughter told her mother that everything was okay and she suffered no pain."

Montague added that the young girl escaped her captor three years later.

I kept this line going, "But isn't that just the power of suggestion in a sense? Her subconscious wanted to hear those words, a kind of protective medicine for the living?"

Montague never took her eyes off mine, "If that makes you feel better about it I guess you can think that."

I couldn't let that one go, "When we come back, we'll have a live demonstration of how predicting the future works."

Yes, you can imagine what was in my ear-piece, Gloria was more forceful, "Jonas, this was **not** in the prep-sheet. What are you doing?"

I turned to Draper and Montague, "This should be fun." I smiled and felt good about where this was going. The break seemed to take forever, not only our long break but one that included a tease for the newsbreak at the top of the hour. We were back on.

As we say, I reset the table, explaining who my guests were and where we were in the interview. I asked Montaque how it worked and she asked if I had something on me that had some kind of personal or emotional value. I said, "Yes, this gold coin I purchased at the Palace of the Popes in Avignon, France."

She took the medallion and held it in her hands. Her face contorted into a trance-like form. My other guest was in her rapture. Finally, out of her small wispy voice, came these words, "Tomorrow, when the sun is in its highest position, someone you know will be taken from this Earth."

I froze.

6.   The Coincidence

When I returned to my office after sign-off, Gloria was sitting on the small sofa with her arms folded in front of her. The body language could be interpreted two ways; either she was extremely angry or she was being guarded.

She spoke first, "What is going on Jonas? I know you. Something is going on."

I placed my folder on the desk and sat down on the chair in front of her. I shook my head, "It wasn't supposed to go that way. I thought Draper would have been more of the defender of realism."

"That's not what I am talking about. Who else did you tell about Ida?" She barked.

Two primal instincts, flight or fight, are important to our survival but in this instant I hardly wanted to do either. If I attempted to change the subject, Gloria would amp up her logic and corner me. If I walked out, I would be dismissing one of the best friends I had in life. With Gloria there was a certain silent agreement of truth at any cost and that had been the glue in our relationship. Gloria didn't know I had a shrink, but I continued, "Gloria, I told you and my shrink."

She laughed, "Oh my God, you have a shrink; just like me."

I tried to steer the conversation away from me, "She's a crazy booking agent, prone to hyperbole." I said, leading the conversation back to Ida. I got up and grabbed a bottle of water from the small refrigerator in the corner of the office.

Gloria picked up her clipboard and made a note. She then tried to lighten the room, "You're right, I mean, the psychic just said, 'someone you know' and you know a lot of people."

I laughed a bit thinking about the ten-thousand plus people I might put in that category and took a deep breath, "Let's not mention this again."

She nodded, "Yeah, what can happen?"

I added, "Yes, like that guy who predicted the end of the Earth. He looked pretty foolish the next day."

"Yeah, he just died!" Gloria remembered.

She got off the couch and walked toward the door, turned and said, "I really love working with you, Jonas. There is always something new and surprising. The unpredictability is what makes it so intriguing. This is the best job I have ever had."

An uncontrollable smile came over my face. She always knew how to break the tension in the room and get us back on track. As the door closed, I thought about how far I'd come and how much I had accomplished. Not because I am so great but because of strong-willed people who could keep pace with my needs to achieve at breakneck speeds. People who could deal with my stubborn Taurus stance on issues always energize me. I laughed to myself. I don't even believe in astrology, but I reference it to explain me. The day was done; it was time to go home.

Once at home, I poured myself a single-malt Scotch and settled into my special chair in the living room. The room was dark. I sat there looking out at the million lights of New York City, imagining them as stars, each one, with some group of planets endlessly orbiting their mass of exploding hydrogen. That made me feel less significant, but at the same time, I marveled at how reality is enriched by science. I kept thinking about what we don't know and how we still have many mysteries to solve.

Maybe it was the talk of death with Ida and Gloria that helped the memory surface, that of my father lying in a hospital bed a few weeks before he passed away. There I was, a young man in college trying to understand universal truths and logic and psychology, and of course, how to write a good lead. He wasn't that old but he was suffering greatly from kidney disease. After years of dialysis he had given up all hope and decided to face the music. The song was not good. He had been misdiagnosed by five doctors who kept treating him for bladder infections, making matters worse.

I remember it was right after Thanksgiving as I sat in the drab off-green hospital room. A few personal items were left there by my brothers to remind the old man of where he wanted to be, back home in his living-room, watching football and telling bad jokes. I could see a pain in his eyes that created a physical tightness in my chest, a hurt so deep I had to take a deep breath. The smell in the room was that of a body that had run the long race. We were in the middle of a conversation, when he turned to me, and said, "I've been a good person." I nodded in agreement as he labored with each breath, "Why is God doing this to me?"

I was barely in my 20s and was asked a question I was not equipped to answer. I looked into his sad face and mustered up the only answer I could find in my small brain, "I don't know Dad, I don't know."

There was a kind of stillness in the room that I'll never forget as long as I live. Here was my father, a man of faith, trying to communicate to God through me — trying to ask why he was treated so poorly — trying to understand why his luck was so bad and why he was dying at such a young age — to die at 66 seemed so unfair to all of us.

I realized I was nursing my own fears with the whisky and it was time for me to go to bed. The next day was Wednesday and I may have wanted to send a message to someone "up there" that I was okay, but I couldn't find the words. I also was hoping that Ida's prediction of her early exit from the planet would be proved incorrect. The alcohol in my blood-stream was supposed to get my mind off Wednesday but it only made the tossing and turning all night worse.

The subconscious mind is a powerful part of who we are as humans. We think we're in control of so much but we're often being misled by our conscious mind. When we drift into our dream state, the inner mind decides what fantasies and fears we see played out in our nightmares and dreams. That night, I kept seeing a man in a hospital bed. Only, in my dream, the man was me.

7.   The Reckoning

Think back on your life. There are usually a handful of days seared into your mind. They cannot be deleted. The details of those experiences are so emotionally charged that your memory keeps them stored in a special place, kept for safe-keeping in your three-pound mass of tissue someone decided to call the brain.

As soon as I woke up that Wednesday, I felt all the clarity of consciousness rush back into my brain. Like an intense movie or event can over-power your frontal lobes, the first thing I thought of was the conversation with Ida. I hated to dwell on it. I hated the waiting. I felt the anxiety of time. I could hear the ticking. The minutes were not marching as they usually did for me in the morning; they were more like a slow-motion playback of time-lapse photography.

About 5 a.m. Gloria sent me a text message asking me to meet her at the Starbucks halfway between our places. I didn't see the message until 7 a.m., so I replied, UP EARLY – WHAT TIME AT STARBUCKS? She wanted to meet at 8 so I dismissed my morning rituals and headed out the door.

The large cumulus clouds to the east cast a shadow on the city that morning. With all the tall buildings the light always has to fight the height to paint the streets and avenues. Dark green plastic walls of garbage bags fortified the sidewalk. As I made my way, the variety of bad smells kept me wondering about New York's major export. Where does it all go? I walked into one of the hundreds of Starbucks in the city and sauntered to the counter to order. As I ordered I felt a poke in my ribs.

"Hey, aren't you famous?" It was Gloria messing around. We got our drinks and took a place in the corner. Students were already plugging in their Macs and working on last minute changes to their papers. The city was coming to life.

Gloria, dressed in her urban-combat look, sat there ramming out some emails, then she looked up, "Do you feel the least bit compelled to tell someone about Ida? I mean, what if she is suffering from some mental problem?"

Thinking, I took a sip of the over-priced latte, then spoke, "She is not going to die. I, for one, would love to interview God but I wouldn't want anyone to die to get the guest."

Gloria shook her head in disapproval, "I have a premonition." She started to tap her finger on the table.

I got her attention, "Gloria, look at me. What are you doing? Did that psychic get to you?"

She just sat there, calculating her words, "Jonas, shouldn't we go to the police?"

She looked back at me and I said, "The police? Why would we go to the police? What conspiracy are you cooking up in that overly educated brain of yours?"

She took a large gulp of coffee and turned to me, "Okay, this is what could have happened. Some religious nut told her he was God, okay? Then he convinces her she is going to die."

I laughed, "Is there a grassy knoll involved with this plot?"

Gloria did not laugh but continued, "His plan is to poison her. He conned her into telling you that he would only go on your show, thinking that you would do some big story about this; you know, making God seem real."

I scratched my head, "So we call the police and they stay with her all day to make sure this invisible man doesn't slip her something?" I could feel the tension build and decided to try to quell this line of insanity. "Gloria, I am going to get my haircut and then I'll see you at work."

She looked forlorn. "You think I am crazy, right?" She asked defensively.

I smiled, "No, I love you. You're always thinking ahead. I think this is all some joke that O'Reilly or Colbert are playing on us. You'll see." I gave her a fist bump, and then headed out the door.

I met my barber when I first moved to New York. He's named Anthony Palitucci and I could get him to come to his shop at any hour of the day or night. Tony was a real New Yorker with a talkative nature that I found quite refreshing in the face of all the blowhards on the corporate level. Tony always told it like it is and he made a lot of sense. In the middle of my haircut I asked him, "Tony, if God walked into your shop and sat down in that chair over there and you had one question to ask him, what the question would be?"

He stopped cutting and brushed some hair off my shoulders. "Well, Mr. B that is a great question. I guess I would ask the Almighty, 'How am I doing, Lord?' and wait for an answer." He resumed cutting and talked about the new mayor and how he had screwed up the school system.

He went on a rant denouncing the fact that the government has anything to do with schools. "You know in my day, Jo, the church ran the schools. Those were the days." He started humming the tune of some old standard.

I was back in the office and our meeting got underway. The silliness of the morning had faded away and we were chatting with the standards and practices people — read: lawyers — about what we could air that night when we interviewed a man who claimed the government spied on him and kidnapped his wife. Her body was found in the East River and the paranoid husband was on trial for the murder. We did a deal with the attorney general's office so we could have him on the show live.

We worked through lunch on the formatting of the show and the question list. Someone had sent out for sandwiches from the Carnegie Deli. As we slapped on the mustard, Gloria's phone started to vibrate. She looked down then punched the messenger icon. She read a text. Her eyes darted back and forth across her screen. She typed something quickly and then read more. She got up and walked slowly toward me. Without saying a word, she placed her phone in front of my face. There in clear print, a text: Ida Pearlstein - collapsed at Sardi's - being rushed to

43

hospital, more when I get it O.M.G. Gloria's face was white. She walked out of the room.

8. The Funeral

It was a dark, dank, rainy Friday morning. Death and funerals seem to invite that kind of weather. A burial on a sunny day just doesn't feel right; it's a misalignment of emotion and scenery. Most of the time, I can deal with death and put the inevitable in the proper perspective. You are born, you live and, if lucky, you make the most out of the time you have. This time I had the unnerving feeling that I was in some way connected to the cause of death.

Every culture has conventions when it comes to death and burial. According to Jewish custom, burial should take place as soon as possible after death. Ida Pearlstein's family blocked an autopsy. They were very concerned about her comments to friends about wanting to be cremated. With the Sabbath starting at sundown on Friday they moved quickly to put our old friend into the ground.

It was a bit uncomfortable running into Dr. Brickman as I left the funeral home, "Doctor, how are you?"

He gazed at me with a look of loss I had not seen before, "It's very sad." I waited for him to continue. Rain started to fall and we put up our umbrellas. He looked me squarely in the eyes, "Coincidence. It's just a coincidence, Jonas." He slowly walked toward the east, I to the west.

I promised Gloria that I would mention Ida's prediction of her demise to the medical examiner.

I had interviewed him a few years ago about bodies of prostitutes that were popping up every other day in the Far Rockaway section of New York.

Dr. Takayuda listened intently to my story and shook his head, "Did you know she had heart disease?" I knew that she drank and smoked and lived a sedentary lifestyle but the religious customs and laws would keep the real reason for her death a mystery. The coroner added before I left his office, "You know, Mr. Bronck, some people predict their death. It's almost like they have connection to the big guy upstairs."

When I got back to the office there was Gloria, dressed in black, her hair pulled back tightly. She was anxious to know how the conversation went with Dr. Takayuda.

I sipped water from a plastic bottle and looked at her, "They are using less and less plastic in these things. I had one the other day that couldn't even stand up."

She furrowed her brow, "Jonas, what did he say?"

"Well, it seems that in a city of 10 million, everyone is connected in some strange way, like a village. The medical examiner knows her personal doctor," I said.

Gloria made a note, "And?"

I wanted to move this out of conspiracy mode, "And, her medical doctor said that she was suffering from heart disease. We just didn't know it."

Gloria pressed, "So, he isn't going to perform an autopsy? What about the prediction?"

I took off my reading glasses, "The family didn't want that and I am sure Takayuda doesn't believe there was any foul play." I walked closer to her and lowered my voice, "You are right, we have to find out what happened."

Gloria smiled, "Okay, after we find out about it we can schedule that big guest she promised?"

I walked back behind my desk, picked up a newspaper and said, "We're just going to have to wait for some sign. You know he works in mysterious ways, right?"

Gloria made another note and got up to leave. "Well, if he knows everything, then he'll know how important it is to us that he appear during the ratings sweeps." She said, and then closed my door.

I always felt death was a little like that door. Once you get to the other side you don't come back. Death is final. I've never heard from anyone who checked out. As much as I wanted to believe that life should have some purpose, I couldn't really comprehend a place where we go after we die. I had never before heard of anyone who had predicted his death down to the minute. What was bothering me was that the reason Ida had revealed this terrible event was connected to something she thought would benefit me, like an old rich uncle passing away and leaving money.

I remember my first confrontation with death. I was about 7 years old and woke early one morning to the ringing of our old black telephone. My mother answered, "Yes, Yes, Oh no, okay. Yes, I understand. We're on the way."

I could hear my father come out of deep sleep and ask, "Who was that?"

My mother, already up and pulling drawers said, "The hospital; they said Mom has taken a turn for the worse."

It wasn't until I arrived home for lunch that I began to understand what that meant. My aunt, uncle, mother and father were sitting around the dining room table. They were drinking coffee slowly and no one was talking.

As I walked in the door my father pulled me into the kitchen and said, "Your grandmother passed away. Please tell your teacher you might be out of school this week."

As I walked back to school I tried to understand what passing away meant but the connection to "has taken a turn for the worse" had been solidly imprinted into my mind. There isn't anything worse than dying. I learned later that the phrase, "a turn for the worse" was just a hospital euphemism for oncoming death. We do that as a society; we create ways of making something cruel seem not so bad. For little Jonas Bronck, it meant that I would never see my grandmother again. I would never have her homemade waffles. She was cold and gone.

Everyone has their way of grieving. It's part of how we manage to move forward. The Jewish tradition of *sitting Shiva*, a week of mourning, always seemed like a reasonable way to deal with the loss of a family member. In fact, the word 'Shiva' means the number 7. Food in the

Jewish tradition helps comfort the family; they are the survivors, after all. Spending a week with your relatives may not seem like a good idea, but as they reminisce and remember all the things that their dearly departed did in their lives they can attempt to find the meaning of life.

Emotionally, Ida Pearlstein was no more than a valuable contact and a unique character. I enjoyed how her old-school ways of doing business actually worked in the digital world. I appreciated her loyalty toward me and how she was always honest. If she had to give the *Tonight Show* the guest first, she let me know. She played the whole board. She never seemed that religious to me. Maybe she knew she didn't have much time due to her medical condition and was trying to figure out how she was going to deal with meeting her maker. Maybe that is why she thought she could deliver the Almighty himself to our show, a fantasy driven by fear.

It wouldn't take that long to figure out whether she was bat-shit crazy or whether it was a delusion that convinced her that we could talk to God, even interview him on live TV. As skeptical as I was, there was a little part of me that wanted her fantasy to be real.

9. Lucky Day

Right after someone dies, we all get a little reflective. With my grueling schedule of 12 to 15-hour days, I usually slept late on Saturdays. The routine included turning off the cellphone, unplugging the landline and making sure no one bothered me. Unfortunately, I could not turn off my thoughts.

I woke up early and decided to take a walk in Central Park. My disguise is rather senseless, especially in New York. I put on my old Chicago Cubs baseball cap, a pair of expensive Oakley sunglasses, an old black parka and even older jeans. On this day the breeze kept the cirrus clouds moving across the sky like debris from an erupting volcano.

Ida popped into my thoughts as I looked into the sky. Why do most people elevate those who have passed away to that place in the sky? Athletes sometimes point to the sky when they do something good. It's as if the dearly departed are satellites looking down on us. Could Ida hear my thoughts?

As I walked around the Jacqueline Kennedy Onassis Reservoir, I thought about Gloria. Would she let this whole saga recede and evaporate? Would she become obsessive and want to find out what it all meant, like the good journalist she is?

As I got to the most northern part of the park I noticed a homeless man sitting on a bench. Knowing he certainly didn't have cable TV, I sat down next to him, "Beautiful day today."

He blinked, rubbed his eyes, looked up and yawned, "Yes, be better without the breeze."

He spoke with a deep southern accent, so I asked, "Are you from the South?"

"Yes, sir, Birmingham, Alabama," He smiled.

I offered him one of my granola bars. He reached out with a worn, dirty hand, "Thank you, Sir. Do you mind if I ask you why you gave me food?"

I smiled, "Well, because I have two of them and I thought I'd share a bite with a southern gentleman." He beamed. I took the other bar out and started to nibble, "Say, you mind if I ask you a question?"

He chewed a bite and then said, "What's on your mind, governor?"

I turned toward him on the bench and slowly revealed a scenario, "Well, imagine one day you're sitting here and God walks up and sits down next to you?"

He looked a bit uncertain, "You saying you're God?"

I shook my head and continued, "This is the thing; you can ask him one question. What would you ask him?"

He stared into space and didn't move for a long time. Then he broke the silence, "I'd ask him: what is luck? And why does he make some people luckier than others?"

I didn't want to freak him out any more than I apparently had so I changed the subject and ask him if he needed money. He stood up, "No, I don't need no handouts. I'm fixin' to get a job. Don't need your money."

As he moved away I said, "Have a great day."

He stopped, smiled and turned back slightly, "You too, sir, and thanks for the food."

His question motivated me to think about how luck works. How timing plays into much of what happens in a person's life. How do some people always seem to be in the right place while others seem to find themselves in the wrong place all too often? There was a newsman I knew in

Washington, D.C. who had this uncanny knack for being at the right place at the right time. One Sunday morning he decided to take a ride in the Virginia highlands in his radio station's news vehicle. While on his little joy ride, he saw an airplane crash into a mountain. Of course, he was the first reporter on the scene.

When stopping into a city building to acquire some kind of license renewal he once again was at the center of the action. A group of Hanafi Muslims conducted coordinated raids on several Washington buildings. There he was, an eye-witness, and quickly jumped on a phone to report what was happening. This act of domestic terrorism was unlucky for the people who were killed that day but extremely fortunate for this newsman's career.

As I walked back to the West Side and my apartment, my mind traveled back to the studio. For workaholics, the next big show is our conscious priority. I thought about Ida's offer of that special guest and how I would handle an opportunity of that magnificence. How would I research for such a guest? Who would I ask for advice?

There would be so many questions to ask a Supreme Being with infinite knowledge, unlimited power, perfect goodness and omnipresence. I wondered how a mere mortal could have the courage to be in the same room with such a power. I've interviewed multi-billionaires, kings and queens and Nobel Prize winners, but sitting down with a deity was certainly way above my pay grade.

As I entered the lobby of my building, I mentally returned to reality, leaving illusionary thinking in the park with the homeless guy on the bench. I kept reminding myself that an interview like this would never happen. Something like that couldn't happen in a million years, a billion years… or even, 13.7 billion years, the age of planet Earth.

10.   Absolutes

Sunday, the seventh day of the week, is the day that God rested. I've always been puzzled why a super, all-powerful being would need to rest but that did help determine that we all needed a day of rest. In the Bible, they were taking about the Sabbath, which in the Jewish calendar is Saturday, not Sunday. In my secular viewpoint, I always regarded Sunday as a time to learn something and have a great brunch. After brunch I would start to think about the coming week. Who would be on the show and how I would prepare for each interview.

One of the great things about the Internet, besides connecting the whole world, is the amount of quality content that can be found on it. In 1984, what was to be a one-time event became a digital, cultural source of intelligence; they call them TED Talks. For someone like me, who could never attend every conference, being able to hear an 18 minute presentation from someone you've never met but plan to interview on live TV, TED was the perfect research tool.

One of my scheduled guests for the upcoming week was the famous writer, Amy Tan. You probably remember her best seller *Joy Luck Club*. I was able to find her 2008

TED Talk *Where does creativity hide?* in which she walked us through how she thinks and writes. One of her sentences caught me, something about absolutes. I stopped the computer and played that excerpt again. She said, "There are no absolute truths. There are never complete answers." I thought about how I would try so hard to question everything and work to pry a fantastic story out of everyone I interview. I always felt that some embedded truth was in every person. In many cases, there isn't an illuminating new aspect of a famous person. In short, sometimes what you see is what you get.

Writers reveal so much of themselves when they write. Even in fiction some pieces of that person float to the surface of the narrative. When you divulge some character's innocent back story, their penchants, positions and peccadillos come out to play. There has been so much written about Amy Tan's life. I just hoped I could do a good interview.

I made some notes and sent a text message to Gloria, who I figured was off on some fanciful flight to a museum or movie. Within seconds I got a response: TAN IS ON THURSDAY. She always amazed me with how she could keep 12 to 15 guest slots in her head. She remembered where they were staying, which limo company would pick them up and when they were landing and taking off.

When I complimented her, she would always say, "Hey, it's my job." I fought for every raise she got and made sure I kept up my radar up in case she was being courted by the competition. In this business, many people brown-nose the boss a bit to get ahead. Gloria, in fact, questioned everything and never patronized me. I never saw her fawning over anyone.

Her next text caught me off guard: DID YOU SEE PAGE 6 IN THE POST? The New York Post is famous for gossip and they corral most of it on what is commonly called, Page Six.

My eyes widened and instead of texting back and forth, I just called her. "Gloria, what is it?"

"Who is this? You know I'm on the No-Call list?" She said with a slight giggle.

"Gloria, Jonas here. What's up in the Post?"

She cleared her throat, "Let me get out of this cab." I heard the exchange with the cabbie in the background, and then she returned, "They mentioned that one your guests predicted someone would die."

I took a deep breath, "Oh, that's it?"

"Oh no!" She continued, "They pose the question, was the soothsayer on the Bronck Show talking about Ida Pearlstein? Can you believe they used the word soothsayer?"

There was a long pause, then, I gasped, "Oh shit."

She mirrored back, "Oh Shit YEAH! You wanna work on a comment? I am sure they'll be all ears over at the Post."

I thought for a bit, and then said, "We might want to talk to legal. I don't really want to give that crackpot any credence."

Gloria apologized, "I really didn't want to bother you with this but I figured—"

"You're right this is going to be all over talk radio and Fox. Thank you for calling. I'll see you tomorrow."

I immediately walked over to my computer and blasted off a note to the legal department. I knew it would take them 48 hours to report back with an opinion but this kind of due diligence has become the standard operating procedure in our litigious world.

I started to think about what I wanted to say. Okay, the concept of "coincidence" needed to be reinforced as much as possible. I needed to make a statement about how much I respected and loved Ida and really didn't believe that the previous night's show had anything to do with what happened to her. I would demand that the press stop this kind of sensational yellow journalism and respect the privacy of her family.

Then I stopped. I sounded like the typical politician denying the very thing that happened. I kept seeing Bill Clinton saying, "I did not have sexual relations with that woman."

I could divert the attention away from myself by saying something like, "Why don't you ask the person who made the prediction?" But that wasn't my style.

My land line phone rang and I jumped, startled. I answered, "Hello."

The voice on the phone was very familiar. It was Steve Summerville, the president of the Triangle News Network. "Sorry to bother you at home, Jonas." I assured him that he could call me anytime, then he continued, "Those motherfucking assholes over at the Post. What the fuck do they think they're doing? Did that lady really say someone was going to die?"

I cleared my throat, "Yeah, but it was rather harmless."

Steve jumped in, "Okay, don't say anything until we get with Harvey and Bruce in Legal. See me first thing tomorrow."

I hung up the phone and sank into the sofa.

11.   Confrontations

On January 29, 1979, Brenda Ann Spencer entered Cleveland Elementary School in San Diego, California, with a Ruger semi-automatic .22 caliber rifle and proceeded to kill her principal, a janitor and wound nine other people, eight of them students. She was 16 years-old but was tried as an adult. She was found guilty and given what amounted to a life sentence in prison. It was alleged that when she was asked why she did it, she said, "I don't like Mondays." This was the basis of the Boomtown Rats song of the same name, written by Bob Geldof.

That song has become the theme for most Mondays in my life. It is almost as if Geldof has implanted a silicon chip in my brain that transmits the melody when someone says they don't like Mondays. It's the way Mondays are for many people. We aren't sure who designed the five-day workweek but I guess it's better than working every day. The two-day weekend does more harm than good for people like me. We are nearly recharged, and then — BANG — the corporate arm reaches down, unplugs us and expects us to hit the ground running at full power. But in my business, the show must go on five nights a week, we are always reading, researching and re-evaluating.

I'm not one for confrontations. I have emotions and I am not a computer chip or a device. I am a human being with an emotional flaw of becoming a bit of defensive when I know I have done something wrong. When confronted, people often will do the worst things. We may lie without a trace of conscience at the moment. Like your mother would tell you "little white lies" as if they were some kind of moral get-out-of-jail free card.

Albert Einstein wrote about our needs as human beings. He claimed religion exerts an educational influence on tradition. Einstein claimed that through the development and endorsement of certain easily accessible thoughts and narratives, commonly known as myths and epics, writers have influenced our accepted ideals.

On the one hand, we learn it's wrong to kill people. That is an act with great consequences. When it comes to truth-telling, the skies grow a bit murky. We accept certain lies to keep from possible pain or cruelty. Have we really created a secondary set of rules, just as primitive man created a collection of beliefs from their awareness of fear, sickness and death?

We learn lessons when we are children that we keep with us into adulthood.

I was in the second grade and I was heading to school one bright May morning. Spring had sprung and the thought of being out of school for summer was running round my brain. As I walked past the bathroom, I noticed my old man's tool kit open on the floor. He was helping my mother put up some pictures over his throne. The bright red Swiss army knife caught my attention. It was amazing, with scores of tools, openers, blades and blunt edges, and I always coveted it. I popped it into my pocket and started the short walk to school.

Between our house on Baker Street and the elementary school there was a small, wooded area. I walked off the road into the woods and pulled out the knife. I found the saw blade that looked like the lumberjack's saw and started to work on a small tree. Out of nowhere came this voice that startled me. It was that Edwards kid who crept up behind me, "Hey Bongo, what are you doing?"

I turned quickly, and shouted, "I have a knife." He took off and I continued sawing. It wasn't long before I realized there were no more kids on the path and that I probably was going to be late.

As I walked into the dimly lit hallway, the first class bell rang. There was Mrs. Robinson, my second-grade teacher, standing in the door with a serious look on her face, "Give me the knife, Jonas."

I could feel the air pushing out of my lungs. I fearfully handed over the "murder" weapon. She added, "Principal Marshall will see you after your last class today." The words were like a hot blade going into my heart.

The day seemed to move like the big box turtle at the zoo. Every once in a while, I would see Jack Edwards and knew he was the tattletale. As the last class was about to end, my heart started to beat harder, my hands were wet and my stomach was not dealing with the bologna sandwich I had for lunch. The Wonder Bread was wondering what was going to happen next.

I walked into the principal's office. I sat down and tried to sit up so I could see over his nameplate on the desk. Mr. Marshall was a man who was as wide as he was tall. He had large, fat hands with bulging clumps of black hairy mounds between his knuckles and an equally ample crop in his ears. He pulled the red knife from the top drawer of his large greenish-gray metal desk. He wore those old 1940s style rimless glasses and his eyes were dark gray.

He wasn't prone to small talk, "Mr. Bronck, whose knife is this?

I took a deep breath, "That's my father's knife, sir."

Mr. Marshall continued his inquiry, "And does your father know you have this knife?"

This is where the frail human defense mechanism kicked in, "Oh, yes," I lied, "Yes sir, he knows."

At this point, Mr. Marshall leaned back in his chair, "You know you are NOT ALLOWED to bring knives to school?"

I shivered, "Yes, I know—"

"I am putting this weapon in this envelope." He pulled out a small brown envelope and dropped the knife in it, then licked the flap and sealed it. "You are not to open this until you get home and I don't ever want to see this knife again. Do you understand?"

I nodded and took the package from him. I got out of the office and the school as quickly as I could.

I had forgotten that my mother was picking me up that day, and since I had the meeting with Mr. Marshall, I was late. My mother was frantically looking for me. I remember getting into the old Ford and sliding into the front seat. She looked at me with her beautiful blue eyes, "Where were you? Jonas, I've been here for 15 minutes."

Of course, a second-grader can sit through an interrogation by the grand inquisitor of elementary school but will break down like a little baby when it comes to Mom. I burst into tears and, finally, I pulled it together enough to tell her the whole story. She was a strong Midwesterner; a farmer through and through. She was loyal to the family and above all, her goal in life was to make sure everyone was happy. She was, as always, the peacekeeper. And part of keeping the peace meant knowing when to tell the truth and when to tell a little white lie.

Mom put the bulging envelope in her purse and offered, "Let's not mention this to your father. He would certainly make more of this than it's worth. I think you've learned your lesson." I didn't smile but I did feel a sense of relief. And as we turned the corner and headed for home she declared, "We're having meatloaf tonight. Your father always likes to have meatloaf on Mondays."

12.   Lawyers

Steve Summerville was old school and that was what I liked about him. He came to TNN in the very beginning of the cable news explosion. He was a good writer but a better big idea guy. He always managed to find the right people and give them enough rope to throw over the wall or to strangle themselves.

I never felt intimidated by him, but I also knew how far to push him. Summerville was probably not his real name. Many radio and TV people take names early in their careers to cover ethnicity such as Scarzinski or unfortunate imagery, like Butcher. Underneath that hard cover and beyond that sailor's vocabulary, Steve really cared about people and grasped that great journalism was the providence of great broadcasting. He was the captain of the squad. He had your back and fought for what he thought was right. Summerville always kept an eye on what was legal.

I wasn't surprised to see two of the highly paid attorneys in their gray suits and drab ties sitting in Steve's large office. For a guy who fought in Vietnam and was pushing 70, Summerville was full of life. And full of coffee. He knocked back at least a couple of pots of it every workday. He was a bit overweight but quick on his feet. His gray hair, still in a crew cut, showed you he was still into the military look. His smile disarmed you and his handshake practically tore your arm off.

His office was a shrine to his accomplishments. Photos of Summerville with every famous person in the world lined the walls. He had his helmet from 'Nam, as he liked to call it, upside down on the window sill with a plant in it. His sense of humor was there at every turn.

When I walked in, he jumped up, shook my hand and slapped me on the back, "Sit down, Jonas. You know Harvey and Bruce here; we won't take a lot of your time."

I smiled and moved to an open chair around the large coffee table, "No problem, I just want to make sure everything we say is right."

The lawyers nodded and Steve took the bull by the horns, "Okay, Harvey, Bruce, we have the press drumming up some phony story based on one of the guests on his show the other night; just some dipshit who said someone would die. Unfortunately, one of our associates, a booking agent, dropped dead the next day at lunch."

Harvey, the slightly older attorney spoke up, "Did Mrs. Pearlstein ever mention her health problems?"

I shook my head no and started to talk but was cut off by Steve, "Look guys, just write some official statement from TNN, like: We do not control what our guests say, blah, blah, blah."

Bruce, the young gun, piped in, "Mr. Summerville, what news organization is asking about this?"

Summerville could not stay in formal language very long, "Those motherfucking assholes over at NBC. I hear pretty boy Brian Williams wants to have it for Nightly." Steve gulped his coffee.

Harvey looked up, "We can just call their attorneys Steve and—"

"NO, we aren't going to work that way, goddamit." Steve's veins in his neck protruded. "Just write the statement and send it over to NBC and maybe this will die on the vine." The lawyers were used to working with Summerville and they knew when it was best to get out early. They took their legal pads and their behinds out of the office, pronto.

After the door was closed, Steve stood up and paced. He turned to me, "Hey, anything you want to tell me that you wouldn't have in front of Mutt and Jeff?"

I looked up slowly and shook my head, "Well, it probably means nothing, but a few days before Ida Pearlstein died she told me exactly when and how she was going to die."

Steve reacted, "What the hell? Was that woman nuts?"

I nodded, and added, "But that isn't all of it. She said the reason she knew this was going to happen was because a special guest she was pitching for my show told her she was going to die."

Steve slowly sat down and loosened his tie, "Was it that bitch you had on your show, that fortune teller?"

I took a deep breath, "No, Ida said that God wants to come on the show and do a live interview."

There was a silence in the room that you could have cut with a knife. I could hear the air conditioning blowing in the corner. Steve stared at me with a stern look, "Okay, stop it. This isn't funny. What the hell are you doing?"

I got a bit defensive, "Wait, Steve, I'm not saying this is true, I'm just saying what she said to me. The only thing that makes it extraordinary is the fact she died exactly when she said she would."

Again, there was silence that I wasn't accustomed to in Steve's presence. He got back up and looked out of his window, "Jonas, we really shouldn't talk about this with anyone else. Who else knows?"

I cleared my throat, "Well, just Gloria."

Steve sighed, "Dammit, okay, Jonas, let's make sure she understands this is just, well, just a coincidence and that we don't need to even talk about it. She should just forget about it."

I agreed with Steve and was getting up to leave when he stopped me, "How did she say we would do an interview with God? Some kind of hook-up?" Steve was smiling now and I could feel the heaviness lifting. I just laughed and headed for the door but like a true newsman, he got in the last word, "You know Jonas, if we could have a guest like that on your show the ratings would be through the roof?"

I looked him in the eye, "Yeah that would be some guest. Better than anything Larry King ever had."

"Keep me posted on whether he gets a hold of you; I've got some pretty good questions I'd like to ask him," Summerville added.

For a brief moment, two TV guys were fantasizing about having the one guest no one has ever seen on TV.

13.   The Waiting

Here's one thing good about the quick news-cycles in America. When something questionable comes up about you, unless it's some Earth-shattering event, it's not likely to hang around very long. The network released a banal statement about the whole mind reader prediction incident and no one ran it. It seemed that some mindless politician, not realizing his mic was still on, had threatened a cub reporter. He said he would throw the reporter off the balcony if he asked a specific question again. That became the bigger story.

I wanted to get my mind off the whole matter of God on the show as a guest. So I decided to see what was happening at the World Trade Center. It had been 13 years since the attack and the 9|11 museum was about to open. It was with this mindset on Monday afternoon that I put on the old baseball cap and took a cab to the site. I walked toward the holy ground and could see that, in so many ways, it was still under construction. For many people in New York the memory of the attack is like a strange, out-of-body experience. For months people found the ashes of the site in their air-conditioning filters, behind book shelves and inside cabinets. I remember the story that Ida told me about that day.

Her husband worked on the 72nd floor in the south tower of the World Trade Center. Ida called him to pick up some dry cleaning on his way to work. He diverted and picked up a sweater for his wife. Her husband, Morton, was the type of guy who seemed rather passive until he started talking, and then he was just as outwardly communicative as his wife. He got into a conversation with the dry cleaner about how terrible the weather had been the day before, it was beautiful today then *bang*. Something hit one of the towers.

As Morton walked toward his office, he could see the flames coming out of the building. As he got closer he could see that the south tower wasn't hit. He called Ida and told her about what he saw and causally said he was going to work. Ida screamed at him, "You crazy person, get away from that place!" He calmed her down with these simple words, "Don't worry about me. I'm fine." Those are the last words she heard from his lips. His remains were never found.

As I walked up to the 16-acre park, I could see the twin reflecting pools. It was an overcast day and as I got closer to the manmade waterfalls, a sense of how sacred this land truly was oozed through my veins. The memorial pools sit where the Twin Towers once stood. The names of every person who died in the 2001 and 1993 attacks are inscribed into bronze panels edging the pools. A young woman who was leaning on the bronze panel absent-mindedly placed her purse over the names. A few seconds later a security person asked her, gently, to remove the bag. She quickly obliged.

I looked up to the new World Trade One building and could only see half of it. The rest of it was shrouded in clouds as if it were climbing into heaven. This was the day after the official ceremony and the new museum was open only to families and first responders. You could see people walking up to the bronze panel, looking at names then staring at the waterfalls with tears rolling down their cheeks. It was hard for me not to tear up. They made their way to the museum to take the escalator down into the underground memorial.

I thought about how much pain this place must give people and wondered why some kept coming back each year to hear the names of those who died being read aloud by loved ones. I often ask myself, how long will this tradition continue? I understood the tribe's need to honor the fallen but I also thought about God's role in the healing process.

We all know why this happened. We all understand that it was a small group of extremely radical religious zealots who perverted the intent of the Qur'an. We know that it was the master plan of a major manipulator, who convinced young vulnerable minds that killing men, women and children in the name of God would somehow get them into a kingdom that included sex with scores of virgins.

As I walked away from the memorial, I thought about the future. I thought about a day when these 400 trees would be tall and strong. Seen from the air they'll cover most of what is here. They'll provide shade in the summer. The mist will float up from the waterfalls and one will feel the power of rebirth, resurrection and renaissance. Life will move forward in America, the way it always does.

I saw a mother with rosary beads standing over her loved one's name and I wondered why God would let this happen. Why he would allow so much pain to be inflicted on so many families?

I grabbed a cab and headed back to the office. By the time I arrived, strong winds and torrents of rain had come. The street's washed clean. The miracle of New York City occurred once again. It's a truly remarkable phenomenon that when it starts to rain, hundreds of umbrella salesmen appear with those cheap little one person umbrellas; a wonder for sure.

When I saw Gloria, I walked up to her, and blurted out, "Let's do a week of shows about God." She clamped her nose with her fingers. I had to ask, "Is that because you think the idea smells?"

She laughed, "Oh no, just don't want to get any water up my nose during the baptism."

14.   The Will

Setting up a week of special interviews takes a lot longer than one would think. Gloria tracked down experts on belief systems, writers of books on the subject and, of course, tapped the leaders of well-known schools such as the Union Theological Seminary and the Jewish Theological Seminary here in New York City.

When I laid out the idea a few weeks earlier, I had challenged Gloria to find people who were low on dogma and high on intellectual integrity: Lean toward learned people who could give some historical background on the belief in a God and help the viewer understand where the scriptures stopped and where man filled in the blanks.

I attempted to get Richard Dawkins to give the other side of the story but his people said he was booked for the whole month. Sadly, one of the more entertaining and clever atheists, Christopher Hitchens, had passed away more than three years before. I remembered inhaling in shock when I heard a small market TV reporter doing a story about Christopher's death say that Mr. Hitchens had gone on to meet his maker.

The plan was coming together nicely and we were just about to write the promotional announcements for the special week when I received a rather inexplicable phone call. A lawyer representing Ida Pearlstein's estate called and asked me about my availability for Ida's will reading.

I was surprised, "A will, really, I thought those things take some time." Ida's New York lawyers were able to move through probate court with rapid ease. He said it would be in the afternoon. I asked, "Why would I be at her will reading? I was just a business associate?"

In his cold, nasally Upper East Side patois, he said, "Well, you're in the will Mr. Bronck. I'm looking forward to meeting you. I have always admired your work."

I hung up the phone and looked at Gloria, "This is getting more perplexing by the moment."

Gloria looked up from her tablet, "What was that about a will?" I explained that I was requested at the will reading.

Without a beat she said, "Well, Good Will reading to you."

I picked up on the movie reference but continued, "Why the hell would Ida leave me anything?" I walked over to the phone and picked it up to make a call but stopped and hung up.

Gloria, reading my body language, said, "What's wrong, Jonas?"

I sat down and ran my hands through my hair, "I was going to call my attorney but I realized this is nothing. She probably left me some picture that she had in her office of the two of us with some famous person."

Gloria diverted the conversation, "These promos aren't going to write themselves."

I looked up, "Of course, let's work on an angle. We need a hook line."

"Hey, here is an idea," Gloria smiled, "How about: *God is back and TNN has him.*"

Like a dry college professor, I said, "Keep writing."

It was the week before we were going to start to promote our big week, and we finally settled on framing the whole special as TNN and Jonas Bronck present: *A Week with God*. The sales department loved the title because it made their job easier to sell commercials for the whole week at a premium price. No matter what the subject, it has to make money and the interest in this special really was quite remarkable. When other famous people heard what we were doing, we had offers of cameos and taped inserts from the who's who of self-important, opinionated people.

It was Wednesday afternoon, the day of the will reading and I had a nervous feeling. Would I be embarrassed? Would I know anyone else there? I put on a dark gray suit and took at cab over to the East Side.

The reading took place in one of the oldest and most prestigious law firms in New York. You know they've been around a long time when the current head of the firm had the Roman numerals IV after his name. I was escorted from the lobby down a long hallway lined with pictures of some of the lawyers who worked at the firm over its 250 year history. I recognized some of the names from a series I did on the secret society Skull and Bones at Yale University. The well-lighted "Bonesmen" looked on as the firm's new recruits continued the traditions of the power elite.

As I entered the large conference room I realized my choice of gray suit was the order of the day. I was given a seat in the back while immediate family members sat at the front, near the executor. After a brief announcement laying out the ground rules, a senior member of the firm started to read.

I wasn't that familiar with the names of relatives and their position on the family tree but as the process moved forward I could feel some tension from one side of the table. This must have been her husband's family. They lightened a bit when one of the ladies got the summer camp in the Adirondacks.

I could see that they were nearing the end of the document. A paralegal walked to a small table and picked up a sealed box. The lawyer at the head of the table read the line, "And to my dear friend Jonas Bronck, I leave some of the memorabilia from our short time working together in New York. May he find some secrets to future successes." I heard my name come out of his mouth and was immobilized for a bit. Then I heard it again, "Mr. Bronck, are you present?"

I stood up and walked to the head of the table, "Yes, I am here." A young lady handed me a box, 20 inches by 20 inches by 20 inches. A perfect square sealed in pure white paper. I walked back to my seat as the lawyer wrapped up the reading.

Moments later I was down on Madison Ave looking south, while the sun blazed a trail back uptown. Red and yellow light flooded my eyes. I felt like a child on

Christmas morning. The box had significant weight but I didn't know yet its gravity.

15.   The Box

I considered dropping it off at my apartment rather than take it back to work, but I feared that would be like leaving a winning lottery ticket on the kitchen table. I figured Gloria would enjoy the conclusion of this story. Ida Pearlstein's will was written long before Ida's offer to deliver the Holy One to the Triangle News Network, so I figured this was just a kind gesture from an old friend.

When I got back to the office, I noticed a significant buzz. A plane had disappeared without a trace and dozens of writers and producers were on the phones with the FAA, NTSB and other government officials. It was a Malaysian airliner with hundreds of people onboard. The plane was heading to China. As soon as I got to my office Gloria, like a homing pigeon, flew to her roost in the corner of my office.

She talked rapidly, "They want us to delay the special on God so we can go full force on this story."

I shook my head half-knowing God would understand that this story was timelier. I gently placed the box on the book shelf. Gloria brought me up to speed on her vision for the show that night. Her plan was to have one of our reporters in a flight simulator discuss how a plane could have wandered off course. I wanted to have our new Asian star Beverly Chen, based out of our Beijing office, report live from the airport where the plane was to have landed.

In the world of 24-hour cable news, you always have to balance the need to know and the desire to present facts first before you massage the sensational or conspiratorial nature of the human mind. In today's world after 9-11, your mind naturally hears airplane missing and you assume that terrorism could be part of the equation.

I lined up some experts from our list of preferred speakers and started to sketch out a timeline for the show. The graphics department had already come up with a nifty visual that mapped out where the plane was at certain points in its journey.

The show was almost put together when I got a call from some lunatic the switchboard had put through. He talked in a gravel-tone voice, "Hey Mr. Bronck, you know what I think?"

I paused, and then asked, "What do you think, sir?"

He coughed, cleared his voice and said, "I think it's another deal like Payne Stewart." I thanked him and got back to focus. Of course, he was speaking of the fate of the famous golfer's jet when the craft de-pressurized at a high altitude and everyone lost consciousness. The plane kept going until it ran out of gas. All passengers perished.

The show went smoothly and we even took a few calls from viewers. One Chinese-American woman was complaining about how the airline wasn't telling the families much about what happened. I tried to console her on the phone while attempting to explain how the airline probably didn't know much more than we did at that point.

She said in a very quiet voice, "Well, maybe God knows what happened."

I thanked her for calling and did the setup for the next couple of hours that would be handled by the newsroom and reporters from all over the world.

After the show, Gloria came into the office and we talked about what we needed to do for the next nights' show and speculated on how long we would run with this story. Gloria was on top of things, "Jonas, I think we should push the whole God week of specials until we know more about the search and rescue mission in the Indian Ocean."

I agreed, and suggested she send emails to all the booked guests outlining the delay and thanking them for their patience and understanding. She bolted from the office. I knew she would be there for a while so I thought I would take the box from the will reading home. I was sure it was nothing.

I stopped by the wine and liquor store just before it closed. "Hi, Harry, sorry I am so late."

The shopkeeper was already pulling down a bottle of Lagavulin 16, my favorite single-malt scotch whisky, and walked toward me, "Mister Jonas, that is such a bad thing; the airplane, oh my God, what do you think happened? You think the Chinese shot that plane down?"

I took out my credit card, "I don't have a clue. It's too soon to know."

Harry looked at me carrying the box with both hands, "You need some help, Mr. Broncka?"

I signed the credit slip and shook my head, "No, Harry, just slip that bottle in to my coat pocket. I'll get a cab." He opened the door for me, and like a miracle, there was a cab in front of the shop.

I got home and my doorman helped me in, "Hey Mr. B," He said, "What is going on in this world with planes falling out of the sky. What's next?" I thanked him.

As soon as I got into my apartment, I poured myself three fingers of scotch, put a drop of water in it, and started to open the box. It was filled with packing popcorn, which always gets all over the floor. The first object I pulled out was a picture in a frame. It was a picture of me with all the living presidents. Ida had set that one up and she had the only picture taken that day. As I dug deeper, I found a folder of pictures of some of my most important interviews: one with the Pope, one with Raul Castro and one with Barbara Walters. I smiled and thought about how helpful Ida had been to my career.

I was just about to set the box aside, thinking it was empty, when I reached back in one more time to make sure that nothing else was in there. My fingers touched something square. It was the size and shape of a cigar box with an envelope taped to the top. The note said in bold print: FOR JONAS BRONCK'S EYES ONLY.

16.   The Key

I sat there for about five minutes, just staring at the poorly wrapped box. I remember that Ida had given me a box of Cubans about three years before, when I came back from Havana, after interviewing Raul, the younger brother of Fidel Castro. This was right after Raul had taken power from his ailing brother. I remembered vividly the note from Ida that had been attached to that gift. "This is just the beginning." I had the letter framed and it hung in my office. It was a good memory of working with Ida. But this was a new box with a mystery attached to it.

Some legalistic instinct kicked in. I felt like I should have someone there to witness the opening of the box. The only person I could trust in this matter was Gloria. I phoned her, "Gloria, Jonas. Can you talk?"

She laughed, "Sure, boss, what's up?" I told her about the box and she erupted, "What the fuck? Why didn't you open it at the office?"

I placated her, "Well, you were so busy with the airliner story and working so hard on undoing the God week, and I didn't want to get in your way."

She waited a beat before she engaged, "Okay, so what's in the box?" I told her that mostly pictures of interviewees and me but then I stopped short in describing them, "And, well, a cigar box wrapped up in scotch tape with a note on it."

"What does the note say?" She demanded.

I told her that the note said *for my eyes only.*

There was a pause on the phone before Gloria returned, "Well, then, why are you telling me?"

I suggested she come by first thing in the morning and we would open the box together. I could tell how delighted she was with that answer as we concluded our call. I put the box on the coffee table but then thought better of it. I moved it to the drawer in the night stand by my bed. I figured that if this was some kind of trick, I wanted to protect whatever was inside the box. Sleeping that night was not easy. Like a child waiting for Christmas morning, it took hours to fall asleep. It wasn't until somewhere around 4 a.m. that I finally conked out.

I vaguely remembered the end of a dream. I was in a stable with the three wise men over me. I could smell incense burning and manure. They were giving me gifts but then, the day came crashing into my dream window. It was the screaming phone.

I sat up, and grabbed the handset. I never used the landline in my apartment other than as a means of getting calls from the doorman when the Chinese food arrived. This morning it was Gloria, right on time. I asked the doorman to send her up and I threw on some pants. I answered the door and let her in. "Sorry, I overslept; let me get presentable."

She shook her head, "You look like shit."

I looked at her with a scowl, "Yeah, thanks a lot! Can you please make some coffee?" She agreed and headed to the kitchen.

When I finally got back out, she was sitting on the sofa with the TV on watching the Today Show on NBC and commented in a snarky way, "Okay, I get it; this is really revealing. She gets married and during her wedding she announces her pregnancy."

I grabbed the remote and turned off the TV.

"Aw, Jonas, don't you want to see the wedding pictures?" She whined. She was only taunting me, of course. She knew my mind was on something more important. I handed her the secret box.

She looked at it and raised it up high to look at the bottom, "Ida must have been drunk when she wrapped this. What a mess." She shook it a bit and looked at me, "What if this is a bomb or some kind of chemical weapon?"

I closed my eyes and opened them wide, "Well, let's find out."

She carefully peeled the tape from one side and looked up, "Okay, that's one." Gloria leaned forward, "Why am I doing this? It says it is for your eyes only." She handed me the box then I slowly pulled another piece of tape and discarded it on the floor.

I suggested, "This has to be connected to what she said, you know, what she said she would deliver to us. And if it is, then you will be involved." She sat back and shook her head in agreement.

I got the last piece of tape off and sure enough it was a cigar box. I slowly found the edge of the top. In the old days, they put a nail in the wood to fasten it. I found the nail and lifted it up. The box opened. Inside was a purple velvet fabric bag with gold tie strings.

Gloria leaned forward, "That is impressive. Looks like some royal connection, or antique." I untied the gold strings and emptied the contents of the bag into my hand.

There it was: A key, a strange little key to some hotel room with the number 1313. I looked back into the bag to see if there was anything else. I found, a small note with one sentence, "This is my secret place at the Qenatas Arms."

I looked at Gloria and handed her the paper, "You ever hear of this place?"

She grabbed her phone, "Let me Google it."

I looked at the key and tried to do my best Sherlock Holmes. I could see that the key was pristine, almost like new. No wear on the bit and the bow was clean.

Gloria looked up, "That place is in alphabet city." That is how most New Yorkers refer to a small section of the Lower East Side where avenues are called by letters. She continued, "It has this whole Egyptian motif. That's a bit dramatic, don't you think?"

I took back the piece of paper and looked into her eyes, "Gloria, let's keep this between you and me. I want to think about what all this means and what our course of action might be." She agreed and I reminder her, "With this missing airline situation, we cannot lose focus. We know we can get back to scheduling the God special when that story cools down."

She made some notes on her phone and then looked up, "You know Summerville wants to go full force on this downed airliner. The whole network is 24-hours on the story."

I got up and said, "Yes, he is right. This is a bigger story than Ida's little key trick."

Gloria got up to leave and while she was moving to the front door she asked, "Do you think it's a trick or some sort of sick setup?"

I tapped her on the shoulder as she walked through the doorway, "No, this is something significant. I just feel it."

17.   Understanding Grief

One of the edges in the competitive world of 24-hour news networks is being where the story takes place. The brass decided to send Cinnamon Johansen, a very attractive blonde with better looks than talent to Australia to be on top of the daily missions to locate the pinging black box. I still can't get it through my head why we call something that is clearly an orange device a "black box." But things are never like they seem.

I was now off to China to interview some of the families of those who were now presumed dead in the airliner. I took with me a great photojournalist from the New York Times, a video cameraman, a sound guy and my interpreter Chuang Ho. Chuang was a Chinese-American whose grandfather had come to the United States from Hong Kong right after World War II. He spoke five or six Chinese dialects, three or four local Indian languages, Japanese and Korean. To say the least, he had a knack for languages.

As we landed in Beijing, I reached into my pocket for my passport and found the key. I noticed for the first time that it had two letters on the top, in that old turn-of-the-century script. A Q and A intertwined. The letters were hardly readable but obviously for Qenatas Arms. I shoved my lucky charm back into my pocket and readied my documents for customs. For all they say about how tight things are in China, I have never had problems moving in and out of the country. It was almost as if the Triangle News Network logo was some sort of All-Access pass. But this trip proved to be more difficult.

As you might understand, there were two forces working against us. The first was Malaysia Airlines. They were doing their best damage control. The other force was the Chinese government. They were doing everything they could to protect the mourning families from exploitation by the Western press. I was looking for more than a story of grief. I wanted some personal interest angle that we could use for a documentary on the whole disaster. After meeting with officials from the airline it was painfully evident that they were in a little over their heads. But to be fair, most airlines are not equipped to accomplish the type of investigation that would be needed, let alone to comfort the families of the missing.

With Chuang's help I read through the list of those onboard. I took an interest in a group of Buddhists who were returning from a religious gathering in Kuala Lumpur listed among the missing. This was a three-generation family which included nine senior travelers and five toddlers. There are some significant relics in Kuala Lumpur. Many Buddhists go to Malaysia to take tours of where the locals claim remnants of spiritual masters are entombed. I thought about the stages of grief and loss: denial and isolation, anger, bargaining and guilt, depression, and then acceptance. We saw the brief layer of denial, until the authorities announced that they felt all were lost. The anger flared up just as we were getting there. The families were meeting with the government and the airline spokespeople who had little to add to this puzzle.

Chuang was able to reach out to some of the families and we did a few interviews. It was emotionally draining but we were there for the story. I thought about their belief system. Many were followers of Buddhism, a religion without a God. The foundation of this faith is largely based on teachings attributed to Siddhartha Gautama. Siddhartha was the Buddha, the awakened one. The ultimate goal is the attainment of the sublime state of Nirvana, said to be a place where one has total freedom from pain, worry, and the external world. This ordeal was far from nirvana for the families of the missing travelers.

I asked one mother about her prayers. Chuang tried to find the right words, he turned to me, "Jo, Jo, she is a Buddhist. They usually meditate, not pray."

I understood, "Re-phrase; ask her if she is meditating." He asked and she just started to cry. We ended the interview.

When I got back to hotel room, I got online and researched the aspect of belief. Buddhists repeat phrases like "May all beings be well; May all beings be happy." They're not invoking any kind of outside help from some God. They are simply trying to help beings flourish and be free from suffering. This kindness directed outward was not a remedy for any stages of grief.

I sat in the poorly air-conditioned room sipping some cheap blended scotch and stared at the painting on the wall. I knew that Chinese paintings all tell stories. I made a note to ask Chuang Ho if he could interpret this one for me. I thought about the void a godless creed could not fill during bad times. If you have no God where do you turn to for courage, comfort and clarity? As those thoughts tumbled through my brain, I realized I was rubbing the hotel room key with 1313 on it. Like worry beads, or a rosary I was working my emotional uneasiness out through my fingertips.

Then I took the other side of the equation. If they had a God to pray, they could ask that, if their loved-ones did perished, that they didn't suffer. They could pray for the rest of the family to find meaning in this tragedy. Using the word 'equation' one would think about the science involved. I started to do the math. How many prayers actually do produce the sum of all desires? The answer wasn't so encouraging.

The next day Chuang found a son of two people who were on the flight. He was educated in the United States and his English was flawless. His mother and father had been on the fateful flight after a brief holiday. He explained they had decided to cut their vacation short and had changed their tickets at the last minute. Had they stuck to their plans, they would be alive.

The young man was calm and deliberate, "I know that something happened to the plane. I know the pilots lost control and the jet went into the sea. I have accepted that they aren't coming back, but I have one request. Please find my parents' bodies. I want them back home, where they belong."

We ended the interview. I thanked him and Chuang asked him to sign the necessary release forms. It was a tough week.

I was glad to be up in the air and headed back to New York. The trip to China had taken a little bit of my soul. Imagine someone you love disappearing; that warm familiar smile and those sparkling eyes gone forever. Only an all-seeing, all-knowing God could explain what happened out there. People need more than an electronic ping from the large dark ocean to maintain their faith in this life.

18.   The Plan

The human body is an amazing amalgam of cells, chemicals and water. We attempt to keep in step with circadian rhythm. When we fly halfway around the world quickly we disrupt that pattern immensely. I hate jet-lag. It's that feeling of tremendous tiredness coupled with this disorientation that keeps you wondering if you have forgotten something.

When I returned from the trip to China I went straight to my apartment, turned off all the phones, brought down all the shades and fell into bed. I slept from late Saturday afternoon until very early Sunday morning. After waking, I found myself walking around my home like a zombie. After a quick hot shower, I ran across the street to Starbucks and ordered two espressos. When I went to pay for the drinks I found the key to 1313 in my pocket.

I sent Gloria a text message asking her if she was awake. True to form, she immediately returned the salvo asking me if I was still alive. I asked her if she'd had breakfast yet and she asked me if I was buying. We met at a small diner on the West Side called Metro. She was dressed in a bright red running outfit.

She sat down in the booth across from me, "So, what treasures did you bring back from the Orient, Mr. Jonas?"

I answered dryly, "That was the worst; those families — what a torment."

After our food arrived I asked Gloria about the hotel that belonged to key 1313. She promised me that she would have some more information when I got back. "Well, it appears that the place hasn't been a hotel since the '70s. Before it was converted to a co-op, it had somewhat of a sordid reputation."

As I drank my fourth cup of coffee for the day, I asked, "What does that mean, Gloria?"

She pushed her hair back and leaned forward, "It was an ostentatious whorehouse."

My eyebrows went up, "Why would Ida been involved in a place like that?"

Gloria devoured a strip of bacon, and then added, "It has changed hands several times in the last 40 years and seems to have been an apartment building, then a co-op."

I suggested we run over there after breakfast and take a look. Gloria eyes lit up. We caught a cab to Alphabet City and got out on Avenue D.

We stopped mid-block, then the confusion started, "No, Jonas, I looked it up three times. The address is 1313 Avenue D. What is on the key?"

I took the key out again and showed it to her, "It's to apartment 1313. That's not the address."

She furrowed her brow, "Boy that is strange; Google Maps must be wrong."

We found the address and walked into the lobby. The doorman looked up from his newspaper, "May I help you?"

I walked toward his stand-up desk and offered, "Yes, I am Jonas Bronck and —"

He stopped me, "Why yes, I know you. Mrs. Pearlstein said you'd be coming. It's sad about her passing."

We both nodded and looked at the key. The doorman broke the tension, "Mr. Bronck, I sure hope you take her old apartment."

I was trying to cast aside my jet-lag and make sense of what he was saying when Gloria bailed me out, "Yes, that's why Mr. Bronck is here today. He wanted to see the apartment. Can we go up?" The doorman showed us to the elevator.

In the elevator I turned to Gloria, "How do you manage to pull off things like that?"

She smiled, "Someone once told me if you simply take the authority in any situation, be calm and confident, and you can do anything."

"Who told you that?"

"You did."

I shook my head, "I cannot believe you did it in a red running suit." We laughed.

The elevator door opened and we could smell cooking in the morning air. The strange thing about New York apartments, as you walk down the hall, you capture aromas of the world: Indian dosa, burnt bacon, last night's garlic, ground coffee beans and, unfortunately, cigarette smoke. We got to the end of the hallway and there it was on the door: The number 1313. I slipped the key into the door carefully. As we opened it, the morning light cut through the dust in the air. Through force of habit I said, "Good morning, hello, anyone here?"

Gloria looked at me with disbelief, "You do know, no one lives here, right?"

We continued into the small hallway that opened into a large living room with asparagus green walls. The place was empty except for one Chippendale chair in the middle of the room. It felt like some of the interrogation chambers I had seen in Iraq. We continued into the empty apartment.

Gloria entered the bedroom, "Wow, what a view of the river. I'll take it," she said.

I went the other way, into a small office with lots of book shelves. "Hey Gloria, did Ida live here? I thought she had a place on the Upper East Side?"

Gloria appeared in the doorway, "Jonas, you have to see this."

I followed her back across the living room into the bedroom. As I entered the room, my eyes found the closet open. Inside was a large gray metal safe. The door was open and an envelope was inside. Gloria walked over and picked up the letter, "It has your name on it, Jonas."

She handed me the envelope and I opened it. There was one piece of paper in it with a typewritten note. It simply read: You will return here this Wednesday at 8 a.m. without the woman dressed in red. I looked at Gloria. Her face was a distressed still-frame.

I asked her, "How often do you wear that running outfit?"

She had this look of intense concentration, her eyes wide open, "Jonas, I just bought this yesterday morning."

I slowly walked around the apartment. The silence seemed to last forever. Then finally I broke it, "This is part of what she proposed. This is all part of an elaborate plan that Ida cooked up. You know like those 'who done it' dinner party games?"

Gloria took the letter from my hand, "Or this is real."

19.　　The Calm

My mind was split between the reality of my job and the basic responsibilities of life with this thought that something really incredible was about to happen. The dream of the eternal optimist always maintains a more than half-full viewpoint in life.

It was the same feeling you get when you fall helplessly in love with someone and even though you are moving through the mundane things, like paying the cable bill or taking out the trash, you are constantly thinking about that other person.

When I got to the office on Monday morning Gloria wanted to have a meeting before the meeting. This was not unusual but today she had something she wanted to discuss before we started our week, "Jonas," she began, "I'm concerned about you going over there on Wednesday morning. Call it women's intuition or whatever, but maybe we ought to have some kind of protection for you."

I stared at the morning papers and saw that parts of Iraq had been taken over by a group calling itself ISIS; the Taliban threatened to take back Afghanistan and the buffoons in Congress continued their mindless pontifications. Nothing of what those elected representatives said seemed to matter.

I turned to Gloria, "What are you worried about? Do you think it's a plot?"

She raised her eyebrows, "Well, it could be something sinister. Like one of the other networks setting you up in this empty apartment with a hooker."

I laughed, "That would be really funny. They tell me I am going to meet the most powerful force in the universe and it turns out to be a prostitute. That would help my career."

Gloria persisted, "Well, I know this private detective who —"

"I would have thought you would be suggesting a wire or a secret camera, you know, something to capture this event?"

She smiled, "Okay, Okay, I'll go there. If I am not there, I would certainly like to be able to verify that you are not totally off-your-rocker."

So, we agreed that I would carry a briefcase with a built-in camera, the kind we used in the old days for investigative reports. I would also have on me a recording device to capture the audio.

Back to my reality: Monday night's show was easy. We did a panel discussion on racism in the NBA. Tuesday night was a bit more challenging. We had the president of the teachers' union, one of the senators who blocked funding for a special education program and a teacher from a small town in Georgia. It started out pretty civilized but flamed up half-way through.

The senator hit a nerve, "You may be a qualified teacher but you are no medical expert. Most doctors are now saying that ADD is just some made-up condition that creates a quick-on-the-draw prescription pad in the doctor's office."

Denise Johnson of the teachers union went berserk, "That is exactly the problem with education in our country. People like you, senator; you don't really care about the kids. All you care about is getting elected. What you just said is a total distortion of the truth. No, better yet, IT'S A DAMN LIE."

The teacher from Georgia wasn't of much help, "Well, I just wish they knew which kids really needed the pills and which did not."

I tried to redirect the conversation into deeper water but the senator was losing his cool as well, "You call me a liar," he sneered. "I'll say it again; you liberals are all the same. Why would we withdraw from a war until it's over? You can see what is happening over there. We pulled out and everything went to hell in a —"

Denise Johnson took the opportunity to interject, "Education is what is important here. Can we keep on topic? Senator, some kids need a little help with medication to keep in step with the rest of the class. Why do you keep trying to undo the Healthcare Act? It's almost like you have ADD, sir."

The senator was not going quietly, "I don't have a disease that doesn't exist!"

I was thinking that World War III was about to erupt right in my studio. Then the opposite feeling, a sensation of calm washed over me. It was a clarity that took me by surprise, "Okay, let's all take a deep breath and remember why we were put on this Earth." Everyone looked at me with a look of incredulity. It was not just the non sequitur, it was the way I said it. I didn't even know where I was going with that comment but my voice just seemed to hypnotize them. I went on, "We were all put here to help human beings in some way." The panelists all started to nod in agreement. I continued, "I have a question for everyone here tonight. Maybe I am having some kind of memory problem but what is it called when you feel like you've experienced what you are undergoing, as if you were here before?"

The lady from the teachers' union spoke up, "It's called déjà vu, from the French, meaning, "already seen." Is that what you mean?"

I could see the senator wanted to jump in, I nodded to him, "Sure, Jonas, everyone has had that feeling. I had it the other day when I met this guy I have never seen before."

I reacted in a positive way, "So, that really exists?"

The teacher from Georgia looked up, "Everyone has that feeling, you know, it's like y'all have been there before."

I sat back, "Okay, so what is it called when you have been on a long flight and when you get back you can't find your keys, you miss appointments and —"

"Mr. Bronck, that's jet-lag, now you do know that happens to a lot of people, right?" The senator blurted out.

I smiled, "Yes, so there are two things that everyone has experienced that make them feel like their mind is playing tricks on them. You want to believe it's nothing but you know it's real. It's a real feeling. Maybe attention deficit disorder is just like jet-lag or déjà vu, only it happens all the time to those who have it."

Surprisingly, the senator turned to the two women, "I'm sorry, maybe I over-reacted."

I then said the most important words in TV, "We'll be right back."

When I got to my office after the show, Gloria was sitting on the sofa, "Wow, Jonas that was smooth. How did you do that? Or, maybe I should ask, why did that happen?"

I put my folder down on the desk, "I don't know why, but I got this serene feeling right before I spoke. It was like someone else was speaking through me."

Gloria walked over to the corner of the room and came back with two things: a brown leather briefcase and what looked like a pack of cigarettes. She handed them to me, "See the black dot on the left side? Make sure that faces the subject. And the pack of cigarettes, just hit the button here and all the audio will be recorded."

I took the two undercover devices, "You know I don't smoke?"

Gloria smiled, "Yeah, but God doesn't know that."

20.   The Meeting Place

The alarm screamed at 5:55 a.m. I sat up quickly, startled by the electronic beeping. I hit the off button and fell back onto the pillow. Then I realized what day it was. This was the day that I was going to get to the bottom of this whole deception. Whatever ploy our enigmatic guest was going to use to get whatever pound of flesh from me, I would be ready.

I got up, shaved, showered and shoved the recording device into the pocket of my shirt. I had some breakfast and made some notes. I have always believed that being prepared was important no matter what you are about to do. Going into a challenging situation, such as interviewing someone like Vladimir Putin through a translator and on foreign soil, didn't unnerve me.

This was an unknown situation. Perhaps it was just a joke that had gone too far. Maybe it was one of the secret camera TV shows, like that *Punk'd* show. I grew up watching Alan Funt's *Candid Camera* where elaborate stunts and setups would fool even the most seasoned professional as well as any man on the street.

With this in mind I wanted to be wearing something that would look good on TV. Not too formal but perhaps something the audience would think I would wear when I wasn't on TV. I put on a blue shirt, some jeans and an old jacket. I wanted to appear casual so if this was some kind of reality TV con I could go along with the deception with a bit of show business flair.

I put on the baseball cap and some sunglasses. It was early June and I wanted to make sure I was prepared for any meteorological occurrence. As I walked through the lobby of my building, the doorman said, "Good Morning Mr. Bronck, up early today?" I smiled, "Yes, going to a meeting. Have a great day." I walked through the front door. The sun was bright; the air was cool.

When I got to the corner I hailed a cab, got in and gave the driver the address. He asked me which way I wanted to go, which some New York cabbies do. I asked him to use his best judgment and I settled down to reading email. As we got to the Qenatas Arms I asked him to drive around the block. My thought was to see if there were any movie production trucks on the other side of the building. Nothing was out of the ordinary.

After getting out of the cab I realized I was a little early so I got a coffee and picked up a paper. It was then that I realized I had forgotten the damn briefcase. I looked at my phone to see if I had time to go back and get it. No chance. I thought to myself, "Oh well, we have the audio recorder." I hadn't carried a briefcase in over ten years so it's no wonder I forgot to pick it up.

I finished the coffee, read the lead of each front page story, dropped the paper on the table in the coffee shop and headed for my meeting.

As I entered the lobby of the building I noticed the doorman was not the one we had run into Sunday morning. I figured this would be just as easy, "Hello," I smiled. "I'm Jonas Bronck and I'm here to see the old Pearlstein apartment 1313?"

He looked at me with confusion. He reached for a notebook in front of him. Then he picked up the phone, "I have to call up to announce you."

I immediately thought that if this was some TV prank, details like this would help make it seem more legit. I stood there watching his face. His eyes looked at me, and then he looked down. Maybe he was new and didn't know that I was thought to be a potential buyer. I could see him turn his attention to the phone, "Yes, a mister…" I repeated my name. "Yes, a mister Bronck is here to see you."

I looked down at my phone; a text from Gloria came in. It read: You OK? I answered Gloria: YES

The doorman put the phone down, "You can go up. Take the elevator to the 13th floor, then go left."

I thanked him and made my way to the old elevator and once inside, I took a deep breath. I hit the button for the 13th floor. The button lit up. I reached into my shirt pocket and hit the record button on the cigarette pack recording device. The elevator was slow but finally got to the 13th floor. I walked out and turned to the left. Apartment 1313 was all the way to the end of the hall.

My heartbeat increased. I knocked on the door. Obviously someone was here. They must have answered the phone call from the doorman. I knocked again. No response. I reached into my pocket and pulled out the key. I looked down and saw the number 1313 on the key. I looked at the number on the door: Number 1313. I opened the door and walked in.

I yelled out, "Hello, anyone here? It's Jonas Bronck. Hello, anyone home?" I slowly walked into the living room. Everything was just the way it had been on Sunday. I walked into the office and said hello again. Nothing. Then I walked into the bedroom. No one was there but the safe door was closed. No one was in the apartment and I thought, "Well so much for this."

I looked at my cell phone. It was 8:02 a.m. and I decided I would sit down in the one chair in the middle of the living room. I made a pledge. I would stay for 15 minutes. It was at that moment that I saw something I'll never forget. Without a sound, another chair, identical to mine, appeared at the office door. It floated into the living room. The chair, probably some special effects illusion, glided in as if some gyroscope was controlling it. It gently landed in front of me about three feet away.

And then, I heard, "In what form would you feel comfortable that I take?"

21.   Deceptions and Illusions

About ten years before, I had worked on a documentary for the History Channel about India, a land of paradox and panoramas. We saw thousands of homeless people sleeping in the streets each night, while large billboards hawked faster Internet connections. We traveled the country and shot wonderful scenes of the Taj Mahal, people in the Ganges River and the wonder of detailed paintings on kernels of rice.

We had just finished filming in the Museum in Hyderabad, a city in the south, and the producer on the project had declared a wrap. The city is located on hilly terrain about 1,800 feet above sea level. As was our tradition, once we finished our project, we had a large dinner with the whole crew that lasted well into the night. It always ended at the hotel bar with copious amounts of whisky. We had been lucky to finish shooting; the monsoon season started that night. It rained heavily for ten hours.

The next day, I took my morning constitutional. I was lucky again; the clouds were still thick and black but the rain had stopped. The cloud cover made the morning light dim. I had a monstrous hangover, but what happened next was as real and unsettling then, as my memory of it is today. I don't consider myself to be mystical, but in the land of Vishnu and vindaloo one can feel a vibrant consciousness.

As I got to the top of a small hill, there was a construction project that I had photographed a few days before, when the sun was hot and high in the sky. That day, much to my chagrin, there had been a young boy working on the project. He was no more than 10 years old. With his award-winning smile, he carried large trays of bricks to his co-workers. Sure, he was getting a chance to learn a trade — but not being in school at such a young age seemed like a crime.

Today, no one was working. The sky was squid-ink black. As I looked up, I noticed fog rolling in. Then, out of the corner of my left eye, I saw a dark form dart cross the street and climb the side of the construction site. It wasn't an animal. It wasn't a person. It was the shadow of the young boy. But the motion of the figure was jerky, like a bad film effect.

In a blink of an eye, I thought, "The angel of death." My primal pre-wired mind massaged by the brainwashing of early Sunday school classes and late night black and white movies, poured forth without warning. I walked faster back to the house the production company had rented for our project. Eight of us were staying in this mansion in a rich suburb called Jubilee Hills. The neighborhood was well-fortified. After all, the chief minister of the state lived one block from our house.

As I walked back to house, strange connections, concoctions and creeds floated to the surface of my brain. I immediately had the feeling that someone in the house was in trouble. Again, trying to brush it out of my whisky-plastered brain, I stopped short of the driveway. There, in the drive, was a hospital vehicle. I moved past the guard and into the living room. Our B-cameraman, Phil Stone, was on the floor. The EMS personnel were loading him onto the stretcher. I asked, "What happened?"

One of the emergency medical guys looked up, "We just need to get him to hospital." Phil did not look good. There was a slight bit of panic and worry from everyone in the house. They took Phil away.

Later that morning, we learned he had had a major heart attack and that, had they not gotten him to the hospital within the hour, our friend would have been a goner. The good news, he recovered and was sent back to the States.

Of course he had to stop chain-smoking and devouring rich foods. After losing 60 pounds, he seemed to be doing fine.

When I asked the crew what had happened that morning, one of the assistant directors gave me this tidbit to chew on. She said, "Phil was in the kitchen making some coffee, when he saw someone or something walking through the living room." I looked into her eyes and could see a little tear coming up, she continued, "He said he walked into the living room to see what it was. He said it was some dark object, like a shadow. Then he grabbed his chest and fell to the floor."

I just nodded and said, "Well, you know we all had too much to drink last night."

Now, here I was ten years later, sitting in an empty apartment looking down at a chair that had just flown in from another room. The words, "In what form would you feel comfortable that I take?" ran around my brain.

I got up and moved to where I had just seen the chair fly in from. The den was empty. I then came back into the living room. I waited in silence. I was sure someone would give up the illusion. I listened closely for a breath, something that would explain what just happened. The only thing I heard was car horns and sirens from outside. I sat back and stared at the other chair. I reached down and touched the chair. I lifted it up to see if there were any flying devices under it, or cameras, or wires or something that would explain how this trick was accomplished. I put the chair back down and sat for about 20 seconds in silence. The feeling of India came back to me. That feeling that something or someone was trying to tell me something. Then I heard the words again, "In what form would you feel comfortable that I take?"

I could tell the words were coming from the chair in the approximate area of where someone's head would be. I took a deep breath and blurted out, "Clever deception, my friend." There was nothing but silence. Then I asked what people have directed to the heavens since we first stood upright, "Now *who* are you? And, *what* do you want?"

22.   Sleight of Hand

For someone who would prefer to live in the world of objective realities, this was not a situation I felt comfortable with at all. I cannot imagine what Moses felt the first time God spoke to him. There he was grazing Jethro's flock, and he heard God tell him to take off his sandals because he stood on holy ground. The words came out of a burning bush. Here I was, looking at a chair.

What went through Muhammad's mind when, according to Islam, he was visited in a cave called Hira by the Archangel Gabriel who revealed to him a verse from the Qur'an. In this retreat near Mecca he was commanded to recite the first lines of the Qur'an. Was he afraid, or was he curious about what was to come next? It must have been beyond description. Here I was, considering what to say to a talking chair.

I looked out of the window. The sun had just gotten above the building next door and a thin slice of sunlight slid into the room. I saw the dust in the air, like stars in the universe whirling around in an invisible current. This could have been a trick, a prank, but I didn't feel I was in harm's way. If anything, I felt an extreme peace. On any normal morning, I would have been up to my third or fourth cup of coffee. But today, I was alert and ready without the extra java. I leaned forward, "As the Bible says, the Lord works in mysterious ways."

I waited for something. It was a micro-second later that I heard these full deep tones, "That was never said in the Bible."

At this point, I felt like, whoever was behind this scam, I had connected to them. They could respond. I do have a reasonable awareness of biblical text. I had done a special on misquoted phrases or misattributed text from the Bible on one of my shows. I had either just attempted to stump the trickster, or had just challenged God.

I sat back comfortably, "Okay," I conceded, "You know the Bible, but I have this feeling there is some kind of ruse going on here."

There was a pause, then again, the calm, warm, male voice said, "You have the phrase printed on your money, In God We Trust."

I opened my eyes wide and thought where is this going, "Okay, yes, a phrase that was added to our money during the civil war. You know how religious Abraham Lincoln was?"

I stopped and thought how absurd that statement was, if this really was God, did I really just remind him of what kind of a guy our 16th President was?

The talking chair continued, "If you trust in God, then why are you recording my words with that device in your pocket?"

I was bowled over. I quickly pulled the cigarette pack recorder out and turned it off. "Sorry, I thought, well, we thought—"

The voice again, "That's fine. I understand. We need to trust each other if I am going to go on TV to be interviewed."

Suddenly, I was reminded of the original purpose of the meeting. God wasn't here to trade biblical references. We were attempting to establish the parameters of an interview. I was here to do my job. I could see Ida at the Indian restaurant the first time she put forth the proposition of the guest of a lifetime. I settled into the game. Let's see where this goes, I thought. I was still a bit puzzled. There was no speaker on the chair but the voice was clearly coming from the chair.

I looked at the seat and laughed out loud, "You know, this talking to a chair routine was already done by

Clint Eastwood at the Republican convention, but that didn't really work. I can't interview a chair on TV."

There was a pause, then he said again, "In what form would you feel comfortable that I take?"

I had been reading lots of books working on the ideas for the week of God shows and I kept hearing the opinion of many that God cannot take a form we would know or understand. And, of course, the followers of Islam hold that one shouldn't speak his name or even try depicting him in anyway.

I knew that this was not going to be normal in any way. I kept thinking, "Don't get sucked into this hoax." Don't be fooled like that 1986 TV show called *The Mystery of Al Capone's Vaults,* when commentator Geraldo Rivera embarrassed himself on national TV claiming he had found the secret vault where Jimmy Hoffa's body was buried. Or like hundreds of unsuspecting TV personalities being abused by Howard Stern fans pranking the interviewer on the phone.

I reminded myself to stay composed and let it play out. I figured, okay, cameras were rolling and this was just an elaborate scheme to lure me into doing something to discredit my network, or perhaps, myself. Who knew? It could be the work of some disgruntled ex-coworker as payback for something I didn't even recall doing. I thought long and hard, time didn't seem to matter with this form in front of me.

I said, "Well, what do you suggest? What do I call you? And when do you think we're going to be able to go on the air?"

Then, a gray block of stone appeared on the chair. It was about 18 inches tall, 9 inches wide. A small monolith of sorts, like the one the monkeys go crazy around in the movie *2001: A Space Odyssey.* Now I felt a pang of pain in my chest, a burst of blood flowed through my heart. Adrenaline pumped through my veins. I was afraid. The room felt as if all the air had been sucked out of the space.

I took a gulp, "Okay," I said. "That's different. But why that?"

God explained, "Those are only molecules and those elements are the same ones that came together to create the Earth."

I took a breath, "And?"

God didn't speak; he showed me how they could be transformed. The molecules of the monolith slowly started to move. I saw them move and reform into Albert Einstein, sitting in the chair. Before I could react, the molecules churned and within seconds became Adolf Hitler. I couldn't breathe. As quickly as those men of the past were conjured up they faded away. Then a candle appeared. The wick burned brightly and danced. The candle faded away. I could smell smoke. And then the chair across from me faded away. There was stillness in the room. The feeling of being in a vacuum subsided and the air returned to the room. I took a deep breath.

I leaned back in my chair and waited for what seemed like minutes and then heard, "Come back tomorrow, same time."

I got up and walked out of the apartment.

23.   Plausible Deniability

I have always had a bit of revulsion for the term *plausible deniability*, which was cooked up by the CIA in the early 1960s. It was code, in a way, to describe the act of withholding information from elected officials in order to protect the agency from any repercussions in the event illegal or unpopular activities of the agency became public knowledge. It was born of the "covert operations" of the Truman administration.

This whole scenario of God deciding to talk to me had seemed more like some movie plot than something that could really happen. There are two wonderful words in our language: overt and covert. Their Latin roots mean *open* and *cover*. I opened the box and there seemed to be no going back. At the same time, I had no desire to cover up this whole matter.

I often wondered if those people who have had encounters with other-worldly entities spent any time considering if anyone would believe them. Did Joseph Smith, the man who dictated the Book of Mormon under the cover of a blanket, really believe that no one would ask to see the golden plates? His followers believed he was a prophet of God. Or was Smith just another revisionist with a quest to change the original word of God into what he thought was the truth?

The only person I truly trusted with my feelings and thoughts was Gloria. I also wanted to have some kind of "plausible deniability" if this turned out to be a scam. I would deny that this talking to God was real. But for some reason, I kept hoping this wasn't some kind of hoax leading me over the edge. When I got to the office, Gloria was not there. I asked some of the team in what we called the "writer's pit" if they had seen her. They reminded me that she had a doctor's appointment. I went back to my office.

Once in front of my giant monitor I googled who owned the apartment building where my life had taken a turn to the bizarre. In the result, I saw that the building, as Gloria had mentioned, had changed hands several times in the last 40 years. But the most recent change caught my eye. In 2011, a company took control of the building and made some significant changes to the structure of the co-op. The article wasn't clear about the changes, but did mention several hearings at the housing board. The company had offices in Dubai and had taken some heat because of their anti-female employment practices.

At this point, Gloria burst through the door with the determination of a bull, "So, what happened? Why didn't you call me? Do you have the recorder?"

I looked up and smiled, "You aren't going to believe any of this, but I forgot the briefcase. And in the middle of the discussion he asked me to turn off the recorder." I handed her the device.

She found the 0001 file on the recorder, plugged it into the playback unit on the desk and hit the play button. She listened to the recording until she heard, "If you trust in God, then why are you recording my words with that device in your pocket?" and then the recording stopped.

"Why does the voice sound familiar?" She asked.

I shook my head, "I don't know but you are only getting part of the picture."

She sat down in front of me, "Okay, Jonas you have to lay it out. I want to know everything that happened."

I calmly answered, processing every word like I was on the witness stand, "Okay, let's get some coffee and start to document the event like a scientific experiment."

While fires blazed in the drought-burdened west, and tornados and floods forced Americans to leave their homes in the Midwest, there Gloria and I were planning a week of shows on God. The entire week was filled with experts with the more dynamic guests scheduled for Monday and Thursday. Monday to begin the week with a bang and Thursday was to help boost the ratings and maintain interest. We still did not have anyone for Friday the 13th. Maybe we could get my new flying chair to appear in that slot?

We decided to keep a special white board, much as the police do when they are trying to solve a crime. The white board would be in my locked office so that our co-workers wouldn't think we had totally lost it. I wasn't quite sure if I were living in the present or just moving through a dream sequence in someone's movie. Gloria was demanding and relentless. She started the process by taking command of the dry erase pen. As they say, the person who writes the details of day or the minutes of the meetings controls the facts for the future.

As I spoke she wrote: Flying chair – same as the first one… Voice only… She stopped and turned, "Why would God be worried about you recording his voice? This is the problem with all the prophets; all the connections to God have had so much secrecy and deception? It's always one person and always a man. Why are the first encounters always with a man and why are there no witnesses?" She asked.

I took out a new notebook from my desk and wrote on the front: **If God could talk...** I open it up and started to take notes, "Gloria, I think the trust thing is important. As you know with any guest, they have to have enough trust in you to take the plunge into coming on national TV and being asked questions that haven't been rehearsed. If we keep this purposeful, as if we're vetting a normal guest, we'll be better off. We need to gain the guest's trust before we get them on the air."

Gloria's eyes perked up, "Oh you devil — ah, that didn't come out right, but what I meant is, you are thinking about God filling the Friday the 13th slot, aren't you?"

I smiled, "Yes Gloria, you got me."

She made a note on the white board, Friday the 13th. I relived every second I could remember from the morning. She wrote quickly and then backed away from the board.

"The baby monolith, Albert Einstein, Adolf Hitler and a burning candle. Do you think there are hidden meanings in these forms?" she asked.

I rubbed my chin. When I was a kid shoveling snow with a friend, I accidentally took a major slash from his shovel. I ended up with six stitches in my chin and a small scar. When the weather changes or I get tense the scar tissue gets itchy. Even after years and years, it is my involuntary tell, like those of bad poker players.

I leaned back in my chair, "Gloria, I think this force, or God or Supreme Being, is in conflict with how to present itself. I'm just thinking out loud here, but if you are totally aware of everything that occurs, wouldn't you also be aware of the informed human mind and want to compensate for our modern-day suspicions?"

Gloria shook her head, "But let's read him," she said. "I am sure everything he did in that room he did for a reason."

I nodded, "Okay, the monolith, he explained it. It was just the way to start the demonstration of his awesome power."

"It's the baby-big-bang, I get it. It represents the beginning of the Earth," she said, then wrote in big letters on the board. "God is not a human form? Wouldn't that mean that God did not make us in her image? I even hate using the term 'her.' We've all been fucking brainwashed."

I walked over to the white board and took a marker and underlined Albert Einstein's name, "I remember reading a short paper Einstein wrote on religion and science," I said.

Gloria sat down in a chair, "And what was that all about?"

I opened my phone, "I'm sure I still have it here. Ah, yes, he was talking about how religion and science's coexistence is more like a battlefield than an orchestra."

"Meaning they don't work well together," she suggested.

"Einstein's whole point was that mankind has two driving forces, the need to gratify deeply felt needs and the assuagement of pain," I continued.

Gloria made a note, "Assuagement – arcane word."

I smiled and then followed up, "Yes. All the images that God presented are supposed to connect to our prewired perception of things. Einstein said that most people agree on what science is but few people can agree on what religion is."

"Of course, there is no one religion. Therefore, one could say there is no one God," Gloria added quickly, picking up the thread.

"But the goals of religion or God might be the same," I suggested.

Gloria had this perplexed look on her face, "And those are?"

I started to write them on the board, "Sympathy, education, social ties and personal needs — I guess Einstein meant freedom — and of course as he wrote, all these things should preserve the sanity and vitality of the community."

"You don't need God to achieve any of those things," Gloria said.

I rubbed my chin and backed away from the white board to see what we had written.

Gloria stood up, "What about Hitler? Isn't he the anti-God or demi-god?"

I put the marker down and thought about the eight-part mini-series I did on Adolf Hitler for the History Channel, "Many atheists claim Hitler played on their team but for a man who seemed to be so far from God he certainly used the word God a lot in his speeches."

"Isn't that what a smart manipulator would do?"

"Yes," I continued, "But when he says things like: *God the Almighty has made our nation. By defending its existence we are defending His work*, he was going much further."

Gloria stared into space, "He was saying God was a Nazi."

I could always count on Gloria to get to the point very quickly. I had this feeling slowly seeping into my brain that whoever was behind this intrigue was going to make us work for every meaning. It wasn't just a prank; it was an elaborate cerebral con.

I turned to Gloria, "The holograms or illusions were put there as symbolism. They weren't just random. They want us to find a deeper meaning"

"Yes, so when do I get to meet God?" Gloria asked.

I laughed, "We'll get there. I just have one question. The only one I don't get is the burning candle?"

Gloria smiled, "Mini-burning bush?"

24.　　　The Judge

There are things that sometime happen in your life that you do not want to admit. We all make mistakes. We all say stupid things at the wrong time. We try to deny them and if we're successful, we're able to forget them and even embrace our imperfections. If we fixate on our foibles, we sometimes need to seek professional help. What happened to me in that apartment 1313 was not plausible. Was it a mistake to even get involved? I was looping but I didn't run to my shrink, not yet.

That night on the show we assembled a group of experts on constitutional law to talk about the Supreme Court, one of my favorite subjects. A panelist on that show was Judge Parker Lundgren, a tough character of amazing durability. At 97 years of age, he was still working for a law firm in New York, where earlier he held the position of city councilmen, state assemblymen, Superior Court judge and for most of his years as the district attorney of this great city. As DA, he battled mobsters in the '50s, civil rights issues in the '60s, abortion clinic bombings in the '70s, horrible murder cases and discrimination issues in the '80s and tax-free status of certain so-called religious organizations in the '90s. He had seen it all, to say the least.

As we wrapped up the show and sent the network feed back to Atlanta, I thanked all our guests. As our tradition had become after every show when he appeared, the old judge and I would sneak off to my office for a nip to end the night. The judge, called, "Park" by people he knew well, always enjoyed a little chat before he returned to his Upper East Side apartment where his wife of 45 years waited for him. His doctors and his better half demanded that he not drink bourbon at his age, but he knew Jonas always had some Old Grand-Dad in his office. We closed the door and I poured a "healthy" glass for each of us.

I raised my glass, "To you, judge. I admire your stamina, your honesty and your mind."

He winked, "That's what she said."

I started to laugh, astonished that a man almost twice my age could come up with a contemporary reference.

I took a sip, "What if I told you God wants to come on the show?"

Park took a large gulp, then look at me squarely, "Well, I would only pay him union minimum."

I placed my glass on the table, "So, you don't have a high regard for the creator?"

The judge downed his drink, "You know, Jonas, I don't make a big deal of this but I'm an agnostic. I probably always have been."

He placed his empty glass on the coffee table and took a stick of gum from his pocket, "Got to get this smell of booze off me before I get home. The old lady can smell that stuff at 40 paces."

I wasn't about to let him walk out the door without explaining his agnosticism. I know the meaning of the word. An agnostic is someone who holds the view that any ultimate reality is unknown. If God represents someone else's "ultimate reality" then an agnostic's viewpoint couldn't even be called a belief.

I asked Park for a few more minutes of his time, "If I may, Judge, when you say you are an agnostic, have you ever wondered how all this got started? How did all these strange coincidences occur? Some almost seem to be miracles, or are these just the creation of those with blind-faith and years of indoctrination?"

The Judge smiled at me with his cherub face, "Mr. Bronck, I want to believe that something is going on here. I do feel a sense of energy, a kind of magnetic force that keeps things rotating around."

I got another question in, "Do you believe in the afterlife?"

"No."

I looked into his wise, old eyes, "Any doubts?"

He continued, "I do want to believe there is something out there. And that all this work we've done isn't just gone."

I took a sip then continued, "Are you afraid of dying?"

He blinked his eyes three times, "Well, I'm not ready. Not ready to be disappointed I guess."

I could see he was getting weary, so I added, "I guess that is why so many people have a God to turn to?" I thought we could end the conversation there, but my friend had other ideas.

He smiled, "Mankind didn't have any Gods until they could draw pictures of them. We didn't gravitate to one God until we could write words to tell the story of one God."

I reached for my notebook, "So, Park, do you think God is some product of the imagination of a few story tellers?" I waited for an answer.

He put the gum in his mouth and started to chew on my words, "Well, yes; but there was always some political motive in their words. It wasn't just faith-based. You had to keep people in line. Just like Lenny Bruce used to say in his act that the first rule created was to make sure people went outside the cave to shit."

I couldn't help but laugh. The analogy was priceless, "Yeah, okay, how did that work?"

The judge grabbed the bourbon bottle and poured a small amount in his glass, "You see the elders made the rule, don't crap in the cave. If you did, they beat the daylights out you and you learned not to shit in the cave. And that is how the first belief system worked."

Right at that point, Gloria did her knock and enter-the-room routine, "Judge, your car is here."

I turned to her, "Thanks, Gloria." I shook the judge's hand and gave him a warm pat on the shoulder, "You are something else, Park."

As he slowly walked out the door he turned to me, "You know I can't even remember what we talked about on tonight's show. I must be getting old." He laughed all the way out the door.

A few seconds later, Gloria popped into the room, "Jonas, I want to go with you tomorrow." Her tenacity was quite apparent.

I put the two glasses in the wet bar sink and put the bottle of bourbon in the cabinet. I took the notebook and put it in my computer bag, "Well, I want you there. I also want to see where this is going first. I don't want you to be in any harm."

Gloria crossed her arms and stood her ground, "Oh I get it, God comes for the first time in thousands of years and it's a guy's game again. You need me there so people don't think you're a raving maniac."

I wanted so much to discuss it further but I was exhausted. I managed this promise, "I'll ask Him, or It, or Her, or whatever."

Gloria smiled, "Yeah, tell her I want to meet her. She has some 'splaining to do!"

25.   The Second Encounter

The plastic clock radio started playing my favorite radio station; but it wasn't the usual morning show patter, it was a preacher screaming about Adam and Eve and the original sin. I reached up and slammed the off button. Then a familiar voice was outside my door. It was my mother's cheery tones, "Jonas dear, time to get up, we're going to go to church today."

Yes, I was suspended in a timeless warp as all the sounds and smells of a Sunday morning drifted into my dreamscape. People who looked like my mother and father glided in and out of a freeform timeline. And then I was there, sitting in church, the platter of communion cups passed in front of my face. As he passed the plate of glasses, the elder's old vein-ridden hands shook. The little glasses clinked against each other like a wind chime.

I heard a man's voice tell me that it was the blood of Christ. I was bewildered, "Why would I drink someone's blood?" The wafer turned from flour to sugar as the saliva interacted with the substance on my tongue. I hear this was the flesh of our Christ. I again pulled back, seeing teeth biting into a man's torn fleshy body. Then a loud bell rang.

I awoke and my phone was ringing. I turned toward the sound and tried to reckon the disparate realities. My t-shirt was wet. The phone rang again. I cleared my throat, "Hello."

I waited for a few seconds then heard the gruff voice of my boss, Steve Summerville, "Jonas, sorry about the early hour but I wanted to get an update on a few things. I just got back from Brazil; those damn soccer players couldn't win one more game. Did I wake you up?"

Not sure why people ask that question when it's quite obvious by the hour and the sound of someone's voice that they, indeed woke you up. And of course, we always use that stupid joke, "No, I had to get up to answer the phone, anyway."

He rambled on in his bull in the china shop style, until I had to focus him in, "What things were you needing an update on Steve?" I asked.

"Well, I called Gloria and she said you might have something as a big topper for your weeklong special on God. So, that Pearlstein tip paid off?"

I sat up a bit shocked that Gloria would have said anything to Summerfield about what was happening at the Qenatas Arms. I took a drink of water from the bottle on the end table and then returned to the conversation, "I am not sure that the guest that Ida had recommended is real," I continued. I know that must have sounded a bit too mysterious for a table pounding media mogul like Steve but I didn't want to give him any false hopes.

Steve considered my answer, "Well, I don't have to remind you, that will be one of the important sweep weeks, and ESPN just killed us with this World Cup crap and Fox is getting a bit close in your slot. We need a gangbuster week to make the ratings work."

I thought this was a strange call, knowing that I would be in the office by noon that day, assuming my visit at 1313 wouldn't detain me. I just decided to come out and ask what was really on his mind, "Steve, I know ratings are important but I feel like there is something else going on here. I've known you for a long time, is there something else?"

There was an unusual pause on the phone. I asked if he was still there, then I heard a different voice come back, "Yeah, well, there is something. But Jonas, you have to promise you won't tell anyone about what I am about to say."

I sensed that something was wrong, personally wrong. Steve is a smart guy. He knew that talking on the phone was better than sending some email or text message. He always covered his tracks well. I leaned forward on the edge of my bed, "Steve, what's the matter?"

He cleared his throat, "Well buddy, I just got the verdict from my doctor this morning: stage four bone marrow cancer."

There was silence on the phone, then without thinking, without even taking a breath, I answered, "Oh my God, Steve—"

He pulled it together, "Okay, Jonas, I was just making sure that you knew and that if anything in your research, you know, could get me in touch with, oh fuck! I don't know what I am talking about. Look, I'm gonna beat this thing. I got the best doctors over at Presbyterian. I'm going to find a way. Now just keep it to yourself."

I promised him several times and kept saying that I was there for him and if he needed anything to let me know. I hung up the phone and rushed to get ready for my second encounter with this strange force that was either using me… or trying to scare me… or attempting to give me the real history of the world.

The cab couldn't get to the apartment building fast enough. I paid the driver and walked into the lobby. The doorman was the same one who was on duty when Gloria and I first found the place that Sunday. He smiled at me, "Good morning Mr. Bronck. Have a nice day." I thought how strange, no call up, no announcement, as if he knew I was coming.

I walked into the apartment. Everything was just as it was when I left the day before. There was the one brown wooden chair in the middle of the living room. I searched the office room, then the bed room. I opened all the closet doors. I looked for wires, speakers, cameras, electronic devices or anything that looked like deception.

I walked around the chair once. Looked out the window, then I moved alertly back to the chair and sat down. Time in an empty room always seem to move slower than in a busy environment. I closed my eyes for few seconds, then the silence was broken, "Jonas, you have arrived." I opened my eyes. The room was still empty. Then the soothing and confident voice spoke again, "Let us begin our journey."

26.   Timeless

The room felt like a vacuum. I looked around the chamber. Was there something moving? Could I determine where the speaker was? Why would someone go to such lengths for a prank of this nature? I had too many questions to concentrate on the conversation. The voice spoke again only this time it asked a question, "Jonas, are you ready for the journey?"

I stopped thinking about unraveling the way they were doing things and decided once again to play along with ruse, "Okay but how do I know who you are? Or more importantly, how we determine you are the one?"

His answer came quickly, "Oh, the rearrangement of molecules or the producing a lit candle out of thin air was not enough to make you think that this force is greater than the Earth itself?"

I smiled, "Well, I don't want to be a doubting Thomas here but I work in media where we create holograms on the screen to make the audience believe two people from two distant cities are standing in the same room."

The volley was returned, "I hear your knowledge of the New Testament of the historical work the Bible, but I also hear the words 'doubt' and 'believe' in the same sentence. You doubt who I am but you believe in holograms, a pure illusion?"

I leaned back now sure I was being challenged by some Watson-like computer in the next room, "I never said I believed in holograms but I am aware they can fool people. If you really believe you can come on a TV show and make a major announcement and convince millions, maybe billions of people, that you are who you say you are then I am interested in pursuing this discussion," I said.

The voice almost had a sense of humor in it, "Oh you flatter yourself, a billion people? You've never had an audience of that size. But more importantly, are you saying you don't believe I am God?"

Shaking my head, "Yes, that is correct. I don't usually do a very good job when I think the person sitting across the desk from me is an imposter."

He continued, "Oh, I see. So the test of what is real has changed, simple formulaic molecule re-assembling will not work."

I crossed my arms, "You need to give me three things that, shall I say, the Almighty would know that no one else could possibly know." I thought I was being clever.

The voice became more monotone as if it were digging out the information from a large computer database. Then out of nowhere it said, "You were the survivor."

I paused, and then asked, "What does that mean?"

The voice kept going, "You were the survivor at birth. The birth of twins, two male babies and you made it; your brother did not. And you didn't learn about this fact until very late in your life. Your mother told you on her deathbed."

My mind whirled with emotion. Yes, it was true. After my Mom's death, I had returned to the hospital where I was born and managed to find the file. I had to use a microfiche reader to find the information. There was one child who survived and one who did not. I had always carried with me this feeling that I was half of a full person but never knew why until that day in the hospital. The smell of the cleaning product they use on the linoleum floors, the smell of used linen and human waste. I remember walking out the place almost overcome with this feeling of loss; this feeling of knowing that I was chosen to live by good luck or by fate, I struggled with finding closure in the death of a brother I never knew I had.

Like a chess player, my opponent had made a crafty move but this could have been just good research on the part of those who designed the scheme. I scanned the room more determined than ever to find a flaw that would give them up. There had to be something in the room that I had overlooked.

Then the force continued, "What are you looking for Jonas, the microfilm that you appropriated from the hospital? Why would you do that? What were you trying to hide?"

I felt this tightness in the pit of my stomach. I didn't know if I were ashamed at what I had done, or the fact that the people who put this whole deal together were trying to break me in some way. I took a deep breath, "Okay, enough. What is your point? Why are you people doing this?"

There was a long pause and then it started again, "Who are the people you keep referring to? Why do you think that somehow 'people' orchestrated this meeting? Why can't you just believe?"

I became anxious, "Okay, let's play. Why would God appear to a talk show host on a cable channel and ask to go on the air?"

His reply was more forceful, "Oh, I asked to go on TV? That is funny. There are two things coming together here. First, a woman who lived a good life did something of great humanity and care. You had no idea. She had been supporting an orphan for the last 25 years. She put the young man through college. She was there at every step. She prayed to me and asked that she know when it was time to go. And when I let her know it was time to go she asked for a favor. She asked that you get the opportunity to do something great as well."

My heart felt like it had stopped, "Really, why me?"

There was a calmer answer to my question, "Because she thought you would be fair and you would be open to the possibilities of bringing the word to many people."

I covered my mouth with my hand, "Open to what possibilities?"

The voice from everywhere answered, "To the possibility that it isn't too late for humankind and that this Earth is not a lost cause. It's time for me to talk. I must say what is true and what is right and just. It's too late for angels and illusions; man has advanced too far for Old Testament tricks. Mankind is so close to figuring it all out yet so far from really believing. It's time for me to talk."

27.   The Second Proof

In my career, I have interviewed several intense evangelists. I interviewed Ted Haggard in 2005. I was not surprised he had a slimy side to him. The same with George Alan Rekers; I felt something was awry. Kenneth and Gloria Copeland who, like Jim and Tammy Faye Bakker, found a way to get rich on God were more con than converted. This did not feel at all like that, but I had to get to the bottom of what I was experiencing.

I wasn't going to be fooled into believing I was really talking to God. I hadn't even arrived at the point of asking what the grand plan was. This God head was not going to go on TV as just a voice. That simply wouldn't work on any level. I decided to go with what I'd been given here and try to get to the next point of proof.

I finally spoke, "I understand. The world is in a bad way. Shootings every day, people being misled by people in power, wars breaking out everywhere, the poor are going hungry; it's almost like God has forgotten us." I figured that would get some reaction.

He spoke again, "Exactly. But before we get to all the ethereal stuff of how I work in mysterious ways, let's get to the point on your mind."

I leaned forward, "What would that be?"

The voice came from everywhere, "You don't believe this is real, do you? You want more proof. You need that second proof."

I got cockier, "Yes," I said. "You can't just sit there, or ah, be there, wherever you are, and just have me believe you are God."

The voice seemed to enjoy the interchange, "Yes of course, you are a highly skilled journalist; you will need to have three sources, three proofs, of course. Okay, Mr. Bronck, here is a proof for you. You have only nine toes."

I raised my eyebrows, "Yes but anyone could know that, anyone who saw me swimming at a resort. That is not God-like in anyway."

The calm voice returned, "Oh, yes of course but it's how you lost your toe that is important. The farming accident and how you almost bled to death. Who was that stranger along the road who put you in his car and took you to the hospital? You do remember the man in the red plaid shirt? He told you that you wouldn't die because he had a plan for you. You don't remember that?"

Once again I was on the edge of my chair, "Of course I remember him but I never got his name."

He laughed slightly, "Yes, because I never mentioned my name. And when I got you to the hospital, I took you into the ER and the doctor asked me who you were and what did I say to the doctor on duty?"

"I don't remember!" I snapped.

He continued, "And what did I tell you when you were crying from the pain?"

"I don't remember," I said.

"I told you that you had nothing to worry about," He continued. "You will be saved because you would become a famous TV star someday."

At that point in my life I was not the slight bit interested in TV, or journalism, or anything like that, but my memory was returning, "No, I was a young kid, I had no idea what I wanted to do," I admitted.

Now the voice spoke in more soothing tones, "And what did you think of what I said?"

My voice started to quiver, "Well, I thought that I was going to live because some stranger told me that everything was okay. I guess I believed you."

He laughed again, "Yes, you believed a total stranger. Remember what happened in the hospital room when your parents came to see you? What the first thing your parents asked you?"

I thought for a while, and then it came to me, "My father was really pissed off about me getting injured on the thrasher. And then he went ballistic and accused me of saying that the guy who brought me in was my father."

The voice got warmer, "Yes, I'm sorry. That was my fault. When I brought you into the hospital they asked me if I were your next of kin. And well, I figured, I am your father in a sense so I went with it."

There I sat in a chair, in an empty apartment, talking to a voice. A formless force who knew things about me that no one could possible know. My emotional reaction to this conversation was eating away at my conspiracy theory. If this was some prank and nothing more than an elaborate hoax, it had become a ruse far beyond anything ever played on anyone.

I took a walk around the apartment. This time it wasn't to find the wires or the speakers or cameras but just to get a few minutes to think about what was happening. As

I got into the bedroom I pulled out my cell phone and looked at the time. The clock said 8:02 a.m.

I had been here for at least a half-hour. My cell phone must be broken, I thought. I hit the speed dial and called Gloria. She answered immediately, "Hey, you there yet? Did you ask him about why a woman can't be there to see him or her or —?"

"Gloria, what time is it?" I interrupted.

She asked me to hang on then she came back, "It's a couple of minutes after eight. Are you late?"

I assured her that everything was fine and on schedule and that I would see her soon.

I walked back into the living room. I walked around the chair a couple of times, and then I sat down. I spoke first, "What is going on?"

There was a pregnant pause, and then he answered, "Oh, you're asking about the time. That is my third proof, Jonas. When are you going to accept that I am God? When you are with me, time stops."

I was not impressed, "Really. You know the laws of science. No one can control time and space. If you could control time you would go back and fix things like 9/11."

The answer came quite rapidly, "Jonas, we aren't going back in time we're just pausing time. It's just something to help you believe. You are a slave to time and I am freeing you."

28.   The Form

I contemplated what it would take to put up a special cell phone tower on a building where a phone would ping that rogue tower and the time could be manipulated. This operation must have cost a pretty penny, but for what purpose? Then it hit me.

I remembered doing an interview with some fundamentalist Christians two years earlier. The head of the group, called the People of Paul, pointed his finger at me right at the end of the interview, "Mr. Jonas Bronck, you haven't been very nice to us. You'll be judged one day."

At the time I kind of laughed and when the video excerpt of him got circulated around the Internet it surely helped my ratings, not his.

Could this be some kind of payback for what I considered to be my normal interviewing technique? During the appearance I had asked the leader of this group whether he thought they were being just as fundamentalist as the radical Muslims. He asked me why and I attempted to remind him of his cult's policies. I listed home schooling, segregating girls and boys, strict requirements for clothing and his denial of evolution as the reason I thought of his group was a cult. The guest got rather aggravated and screamed, "Who told you that?"

I just continued, "Well, then it is true?" He never answered the question. My sources were impeccable.

Returning to the all-knowing computer in apartment 1313, I opened with, "I know that this probably is all explainable in some way but I am curious about a few things."

The voice came back, "Yes, what you would like to know? Perhaps you are wondering how God could go on TV?"

Again, I was drawn in, "Well, yes, that is exactly what I was thinking about."

I started to roll this scenario in my mind. We have three hours on a Friday night. I am sitting in my studio. The network has been promoting this heavily for two weeks. Every other news operation is asking how they can get a piece of the action. The promos keep saying, the one and only God, exclusively with Jonas Bronck this Friday night on TNN.

I had to ask, "After I introduce you to the audience what do the people see? It's TV." What I am about to type next I feel hardly capable of putting into words. As I sat there a man appeared near the window. He was smoking a pipe. He turned and looked at me, it was my father. I opened and closed my eyes and shook my head. Is this a dream? Am I seeing a hologram? Have I been drugged? Is this simply a hallucination? I looked at him for a long time then I finally broke the silence, "Who are you?"

The avatar of my father slowly withdrew the pipe from his mouth, "Jonas, it's me, your father."

Fear fell over me. My heart burned as I looked at the form and I knew he was my father. I first wanted so much to jump up and hug him but the skeptic in me was just as strong, saw him as an illusion. My mind kept repeating, "Don't get fooled by these people." This was a sick joke. They found a lookalike — but the voice was perfect, the brand of tobacco and that familiar smell. I was being drawn into the scheme.

I took a deep breath, "So, I see you can take any form. Are you trying to give me suggestions on what you might look like for the TV appearance or are you just trying to prove you are the one true God?" The man put the pipe back into his mouth and he took a long deep drag of smoke, like my father always did. Then we both exhaled at the same time.

He turned to me, "I am proud of you Jonas. You were always the sharpest tool in the shed."

He laughed and then slowly faded away, but the smoke lingered. The expression, *that guy wasn't the sharpest tool in the shed* was one my father used often when describing what he called the village idiots. As he faded, I wanted nothing more than to leave this place. A deep feeling of sadness and regret overwhelmed me. My playtime with imaginary god-man was over. I got up to leave the room.

As I got halfway across the room the voice returned, "Isn't there one more question you want to ask today?"

I swung around abruptly, "Why don't you tell me what I am thinking, you sick fuck?" There was no answer. I walked slowly to the door and when my hand touched the doorknob, I could feel that it was hot. Not burning hot but as if someone had been holding it for a long time. I turned around and asked, "What are you doing now?"

The warmth came back to his voice, "You want to bring your woman with you tomorrow?"

I walked back toward the chair, "What are you talking about?"

He continued, "The woman named Gloria; isn't she your disciple?"

I laughed out loud, "That seems a bit arcane. No, she isn't my disciple; she is my producer. We work on the same show."

The voice was playful now, "But she seems to be more than just some employee. She has this great respect for you and she carries many causes with her."

I didn't believe this but had to engage, "Well, yes; she is smart — and what causes are you talking about?"

The Godhead continued, "She believes that most of what has been written and said about me is the construct of men. You know that she is right."

I chuckled under my breath, "Well it does seem that way. So, what are you going to do about that?"

"Tomorrow," he commanded, "When you come back at 8 a.m. you will bring Gloria and we will discuss the matter of my TV image, subject matter of the interview, guidelines, and of course, when I will appear."

I walked to the door robotically, "Yes, I'll see if she wants to come. I guess we'll see you tomorrow."

By the time I got into the elevator I was confused and frustrated. Why was the creator, who I was taught was all powerful and all knowing, playing such mean tricks to make me believe?

As I got out of the elevator the doorman looked up. Checked his watch and then asked, "Are you okay Mr. Bronck? You went up about two minutes ago."

I nodded and walked out of the door. My cell phone now said 8:03 a.m. I walked across the street, got a cab and when I looked down at the TV unit in the taxi the time on the screen was 8:06 a.m.

Time certainly did stand still for me.

29.   The Affirmation

I knew that once Gloria became involved in this journey things would become much more organized and focused. We have such a wonderful working relationship. I tend to be the exposed nerve ending and she's the calculator and analyzer. Most of the best questions I ask on air are being parroted by me after she sends them to me via the IEM (in-ear monitor). That is the way TV works.

As I got back to my job that night the show featured an intense debate between a pro-Israel expert and a former official in the Palestinian government. The night before, more than a dozen people had been killed after Israel launched airstrikes into the Hamas-controlled Gaza Strip. The attack was in retribution for three Israeli soldiers being kidnapped and killed. Of course Hamas fired rockets back at Israel. Israeli's cabinet immediately authorized the military to call up 40,000 reservists. The discussion was another heated exchange between two factions with little in common politically, but anthropologically they were from the same original tribes.

The Israeli guest brought up the fact that the land had been promised to the Jews by God. This sent the guest into defending Hamas and Palestine, an emotional spiral that ended with the two storming off the set. I quickly went to commercial and asked Gloria what we should do with three minutes left.

She spoke quickly into my headset, "I've loaded the teleprompter with the promo for God week. Just read it verbatim and you'll be fine."

We came back from break and I apologized to the audience and started to read the teleprompter. It began with a list of all the guests we had lined up for A Week with God on TNN. As I got to the end I wasn't sure where the text was going. I robotically read, "We have the whole week planned for you and on Friday, we just might surprise you. We do promise it will be a Good Friday."

I did my traditional sign off, "Good night and sleep well." Once the stage manager signaled we were out, I asked Gloria, "What was that all about?"

She answered with, "Let's talk in your office."

The tech took my mic and the IEM and put them in a special case marked with my name. I walked through the green room hoping to see the two guests and sort it out. When I got there, the only person in the room was the intern who said, "Boy, Mr. Bronck, those guys were really sick. They just walked out the emergency exit screaming at each other."

I looked at the intern and tried to make it a teachable moment, "Yes, it's been going on for more than 50 years, and due to their mutual distrust of each other, nothing gets accomplished."

The intern naively suggested, "It's because they have a different God, right?"

"No, you should read up on it," I barked. "They have the same God, the God of Abraham."

The intern nervously continued, "But those Gods have different names."

I softened and patted him on the back, "We all have different names but we're all people. By the way, what is your name?"

"Joseph." He answered.

"Good job tonight, Joseph."

When I got to my office there was Gloria sitting with a brand new legal pad in her lap, "Okay, boss, what is the plan?" I looked at her and asked her if she wanted a drink. She held up her Poland Spring bottle and said that water was all she needed. I sat down across from her and went through the meeting I had earlier in the day in apartment 1313.

She was taking notes and then stopped, "Okay, let me see if I get this right. You get there a little before 8 a.m. and you had a meeting with, ah, God, and he told you that time had stopped. How long were you talking before you called me?"

I once again laid out the timeline, "I was in the apartment for more than 30 minutes talking but my cell phone clock must have stopped."

She took her iPhone out and looked at the time I called her, "Jonas, you asked me what time it was at 8:02 a.m. How did they do that?"

I took my notebook and looked at the notes I scribbled in the cab, "Yes. The doorman said I had been there only a few minutes. He asked me if there was something wrong." I made a few more notes and then turned to Gloria, "He wants you to come tomorrow. He already knew you wanted to come. It's like he's reading my mind."

Gloria smiled and her face went into faux panic, "Oh, my, Jonas, I have nothing to wear. What does a girl from Scarsdale wear when she has her first meeting with

God?" I looked at her with a serious stare. She added, "Okay, Okay, I get it. This is serious stuff. But I have to ask where are you, say 1 to 10, with 10 being the absolute belief that you are meeting with God and 1 being that the whole thing is a total fabrication?"

I slowly answered, "Well, the first time, I was in the 1 or 2 range. But now I am moving into the 7 range. I think what pushed me higher was the stunt with the hologram of my father. It was so lifelike and believable."

I took a big sip of Scotch and started to put my papers in my computer bag. "Where do you think you are going, cowboy?" Gloria asked.

I turned off the lamp on my desk and started to move toward the door, "I am going home. Maybe it's the time-standing still bit or something but I am dead."

Gloria looked at me and said something that stuck with me, "Jonas, I think the most important question we have to ask, that is — if it's the real God — why now?"

I wrinkled my brow, "Have we pushed things so far he feels we're close to blowing up the whole planet?"

Gloria diverted into her own thought pattern, "If you discount the accounts of the Angel Gabriel coming down to talk to men and Jesus and Muhammad's encounters with the Lord Almighty, God really hasn't popped in too much. Why now?"

I answered, "I think he thinks he has to straighten us out. We certainly do need to be shown the right path, but I am not sure this is going to turn out well."

Gloria got up to walk me out of my own office, "Jonas, you know we have a problem if he only wants to talk. No one will believe us. But on the other hand, what does God look like? Muslims won't let us show him, Jews will rebuke us and Christians will boycott our advertisers."

As I locked the door, I said, "Make sure you bring your sense of humor; you'll need it. Meet me there at 7:55 a.m."

30.   The Third Encounter

When I got to the Qenatas Arms, Gloria was sitting on the sofa in the lobby working on her legal pad. She also had an iPad open and she was going back and forth like a chipmunk trying to decide which nut was best to store in her cheek. She also had a cup of coffee on the table in front of her.

She looked up, "Oh, great, you're here, you remembered."

I laughed and came back with, "Yeah, I wouldn't miss this for anything; two Supreme Beings duking it out."

We waved at the door man and proceeded to the elevator. Gloria turned to me, "Do you think it's rude for me to bring coffee and not have one for him?"

I looked at her deadpan, "I'm sure if he wants one, he can just conjure one up."

The elevator door opened and she continued, "Don't think it's a bit creepy that he lives on the 13th floor?"

We got to the door and I opened it. We went into the living room and now there were two identical chairs.

She looked at me, "Well that was nice of him."

I did my routine of looking in all the rooms before I sat down. She looked in the kitchen cabinets. I asked her, "What are you looking for?"

She shrugged her shoulders, "Hey, you never know, maybe some angel food cake."

I stared at her, "Really Gloria?" She skipped over and sat in one of the chairs. I mentioned, "Oh, I usually sit on that one."

She looked at me with this "excuse me" expression and moved to the other chair. We waited for about two minutes; then Gloria said, "What time is it?"

God spoke, **"You don't have to worry about time here, Gloria."**

She looked around, got up and walked around the room, "Okay, can you talk again so I can get a read on where the sound is coming from? The acoustics here are a bit strange." There was more silence. Gloria sat down and decided to be good.

I said, "Now that we have Gloria here, perhaps we should start by determining what we call you."

The voice got a bit deeper, God spoke, **"Why don't we leave it in your terminology, God is fine."**

Gloria nodded and made a note on her legal pad. She started the vetting process she engaged in with any guest booked on the show. She cleared her throat, "Okay, God, we really want to thank you for taking the time to go over some preliminary discussions. These are just casual conversations to help us put together a question list for when we're live on the air. You should be in the studio about an hour before we go live and we ask that you not wear anything green."

God spoke, **"That makes sense but have you determined what physical form I should take when I am being interviewed?"**

Gloria looked at me with this incredulous face, "Well, let's not get bogged down in that right now. Perhaps you can surprise us? But yes, whatever form you take, remember the American TV audience really has seen everything." Gloria continued, "Do you need any graphics? Will you bring film clips or any evidence you would like to present for your time on TV?"

"Is this really necessary, Gloria?" I had to stop her.

"Jonas, please let her do her job. These are important questions."

I sat back and waved her on. "Okay, God, we aren't going to take any calls from viewers; we thought it would be better to just focus on your message and what you are trying to accomplish, which brings me to this question: Why are you doing this now?"

There was a pause, then, God spoke, **"It's time for Earth's humans to know the truth. You seem to have so many answers and so many weapons that can eliminate people from your planet. A visit from God is mandatory. It's time to talk."**

I stepped in, "We are doing what we are calling 'A Week with God' in about two weeks, and we thought we would end the week with you on Friday the 13th for three hours, 8 p.m. to 11 p.m. Eastern Time."

"That sounds like a perfect week of programming, Jonas."

Gloria smiled, "Yes, I'm sure we'll have millions and millions of viewers."

"That is not my concern. I know that my message will get out."

"So, Jonas says he's about 70 percent in your corner on a belief level but since I am the new girl here I have some qualifying questions. As you know, we vet every guest," She said in a tone that sounded almost like a warning.

"Gloria, I know that you are an atheist. You were raised by parents who are physicists. You don't believe any of this, do you?"

Gloria blushed, "You got me there, God. Yes, I was taught that everything can be tested with science and there isn't a lot of room for an intelligent designer when you get around a bunch of science heads. That group also has trouble with a 'Supreme Being' who doesn't seem to have the power to keep murderous weather patterns away from innocent people."

"Gloria," I whispered.

"That is fine, Jonas. She is the best sounding board for the discussion. We must be able to do this show the right way. We must get at the truth. You have to have ask the right questions. We aren't aiming for a show of adulation; we are looking for a show of illumination."

Gloria pulled back her legal pad to the first page, "Okay here goes, the first three questions: Does the universe or the cosmos really exist? The observable universe is about 46 billion light years in radius; is that real; or are we just part of some grand illusion? Okay, number two: Does God exist? And if you do exist, did you make the universe; you know Big Bang and all that? And finally, what have you been doing since the Big Bang?"

My jaw fell to the ground. I couldn't believe she was standing before God and asking those questions right out of the box.

"I believe that is more than three questions."

31.   Rude Awakening

There were no rules for Gloria to follow. This has never happened before in our lifetimes and being respectful was what I had been taught. Where I grew up, we were given a strong view of the Old Testament and God. We were taught the rhyme, *"Jesus loves me this I know, For the Bible tells me so; little ones to him belong, they are weak but he is strong."* That wasn't in the Bible. It was actually from the pen of Anna Bartlett Warner and first published it in 1860. Not everything was in the Bible, but we studied God and the Bible for hours and hours. After all, it is the Gospel — to bring or announce good news. We read the Scriptures and memorized prayers. We were instructed that if we did not respect the Lord terrible things would happen. Terrible things happened, anyway. Within minutes of meeting her creator, Gloria Madoffa had figuratively put him against the wall. I sat back and watched.

"Those are very good questions. I'm not sure you are going to understand it, but I do have answers."

Gloria quipped, "Understand it? What, because I'm a woman? Look, we are all intelligent people here. Please walk us through it. What's the good news, God?"

"The universe is never ending. It's infinite beyond any comprehension of human minds. It is a non-linear event, without form, just a forever, that goes, well, forever."

Gloria was on the edge of her seat, "What else? Tell us more."

"You have just recently discovered one of the most important things in science called Dark Flow. It's a gravitational force from a section of the universe that isn't as uniform as your scientific laws would have you believe."

I jumped in, "You mean Black Holes?"

"No Jonas, Black Holes are good. They are areas that are preparing to create new universes and thus continue the cycle. Dark Flow is an evil expansion, especially for mankind. It moves about 200 million miles an hour. This is the force I need to deal with so that your tranquility is not disrupted."

Gloria wrote quickly and then looked up, "So, the laws of science, like electrical energy and magnetic force and time and space are all there. They aren't just a scientific theory?"

"Your scientists, especially theoretical physicists, are very smart. They are limited by time. They have not been able to deal with it all very well, but they continue to study. To reach the next level of the universe they will need to invent some new way of travel, so they can get to the next universe in a lifetime. They can look backward in time better than forward in time. Every year archeologists find new answers to what has come before, but no human being can truly comprehend the time between major events."

I made a note, "So, we're talking 13 or 14 billion years?"

"To be exact the universe is 14 billion years old and the Earth, as a more stable form, is only 5 billion years old. But remember, that is just this universe. There are one-hundred billion or more of them out there. Mankind's fun is just beginning."

Gloria started a new line of questioning, "What about the people who say the Earth is one atom away from being too hot or too cold to have created life. Is Earth some special planet that received the gift of life from an intelligent designer?"

I had to jump in, "And what about parallel universes? Is that just scientific mumbo-jumbo?"

"Each universe has life. The people of Earth have created a set of rules or laws that say this is what you need to have life. But those are rules you created in your own image. You are a carbon and water planet. There are other planets that are gas and fire-based. That is life as well; just a different kind of life. It wasn't that long ago that your planet was thought to be the center of things. You put people in jail, or worse, killed them because they said the Sun was the center of your solar system. Man still has a lot to learn."

Gloria jumped in, "Why do you have to say 'man' all the time?"

"Yes Gloria, your language is so limited. Humankind sounds oxymoronic. I can only use the words you use to communicate. I hope your viewers will understand. And speaking of words, I assume your question about what I have been doing since the big bang was rhetorical? What do I have to do, let some large meteor destroy Earth?"

Gloria smiled, "Oh, are we going Old Testament now?"

"We will get to that later but I want to make sure that we do talk about the cosmic realities when we are on the air. It is very important that everyone understands how delicate the celestial balance is and how dangerous the universe can be."

I asked, "Is the proper reaction fear? Is this what we should be feeling?"

"No, I do not want anyone to be afraid. I am here and I have always been here. With the discrediting of old tales and superstitions, people may be able to live in a peaceful, kind world. Forget about what you've read. Man has been doing a lot of writing and speaking and preaching about who I am. Only God can say what God is."

I pointed out, "I heard you say 'what' God is and not 'who' God is?"

"Yes, I'm like gravity. You know gravitational pull exists but you don't quite know how it is made or what causes it."

Gloria pressed him, "What is gravity? What is it good for?"

"Everything with mass, from a dust mote to a star, exerts a gravitational pull. But you only have theories about how it is created. I am a force beyond mass. There are things we need to be attracted to and things we must be repelled from to stay alive. Gravity is important, so the moon doesn't crash into the Earth. And on the other hand, gravity makes sure the moon doesn't fly away. The Earth is moving very fast and the moon must keep up."

I had to ask, "And the moon is important?"

"Without the moon, your days would be shorter. It would take almost 1,000 days to complete a year. Your tides would be much smaller. Your nights would be darker. Your axial tilt would vary tremendously over time and the whole planet would become unstable. You could end up with winter at the equator and tropic heat at your poles. The moon is best right where it is."

Gloria jumped in, "Asimov, Isaac Asimov said that during the development of life on Earth the moon was closer and created amble waves that churned up the sea and moved sea life toward the land."

"The moon does have that power. It forced man to count. Seeing the changing cycles of the moon helped man understand the great progression of time and seasons. Counting forced mankind into math and clicked the numbers part of his brain. Once he started to count, he never stopped."

I added, "And then man saw the stars and planets and imagined visual maps, or pictures. They named the collections after Gods of the times - Mercury, Venus, Mars, Jupiter and Saturn."

"People are drawn to mysterious things. They are drawn to things that are good and things that are bad.

There are good forces and bad forces. They need to understand the gravitational forces that are at work. Science has always been part of the plan for man."

Gloria perked up, "But you didn't answer the most important question. Did you create the universe?" The air seemed to go out of the room and then we heard these words,

"I *am* the universe."

32.   Back to Reality

We sat in the cab on the way back to the office in silence. I could see that Gloria was thinking, concentrating and processing all she had just experienced. It wasn't like I was some old hand at this. I could see that she was trying to put it all together.

Finally she spoke, "I'm usually really good at knowing where audio is coming from in a room. These guys are really good. Whatever they are using to create the sound, it really seems like a person sitting there with us."

I asked the driver to go up 10th Avenue to avoid the traffic and I then turned to Gloria, "So, on the 1 to 10 scale, where are you?"

She ran her hand through her hair and looked at me, "I'm intrigued, but I am only a 2. Maybe it's my upbringing and what's been drilled into my head but I don't get it."

I asked, "What don't you get?"

She pursed her lips, "We've all seen people who want to go on the show and there is always some agenda. Even with the best ones it's obvious, they want to sell a book or to hype a cause or a movie. I mean, all you have to do to get Bill Clinton on TV is ask him to come on and talk about giving away money. What's God's motive? What is *he* trying to do?"

We came to our stop. I paid the driver and we went up to the office. I looked down at my phone and saw a text from Steve Summerville's PA that said Do you have some time to come up and see Steve?

I made my way to the third floor and Steve's assistant ushered me right into his office. He did not look well, "Hey, Steve, how are you?"

Steve looked at me and forced a small smile, "I'm okay, just a bit anxious."

I sat down in the chair in front of his desk, "Is there anything I can do?"

This set him off, "No goddamn it. Why do people keep asking me that?"

I leaned back and waited for him.

"Aw, I'm sorry Jonas. This thing is pissing the shit out of me. I'm going up to Minnesota to the Mayo Clinic. They got some highly priced prima donna doctor who thinks we can kill this fucking cancer."

"That's great Steve; really wonderful news," I said.

He got serious again, "I just have to convince my son to donate some bone marrow. You know we haven't been on speaking terms ever since he moved to San Francisco with his fucking boyfriend," he said.

"Steve, I think you just have to convince him that his sexual preference doesn't bother you, even if it still does. Surely, he will help his father?"

Steve pushed some papers away, "Yes, we had the discussion. He just sent me an email saying he'll meet me tomorrow in Minnesota."

I nodded and he looked at me with this look of 'hey what can you do', then he shifted gears, "What's going on with your lead? What gives with this God thing?"

I took a deep breath, "Well Steve, if it isn't God it's the most elaborate stunt that Gloria and I have ever been sucked into."

Steve's eye brows elevated, "You took Gloria with you? I thought he only wanted to talk to you?"

I answered without emotion, "Well you know Gloria, she started in with that God never talks to women and—"

Just then, the phone buzzed, Steve picked it up and said hello. He started to smile, and then cupped the phone, "It's my son, and I gotta talk to him."

I nodded that it was okay and I let myself out. As I was walking down the corridor of power, as we call it, lined with large pictures of some of the most powerful people in the media spotlight, I wondered: Was God already working some magic for Steve?

When I got to my office, Gloria was sitting ready for the show prep meeting. Some of the writers, producers and staff people had gathered around the large conference table. I looked at Gloria and she smiled knowingly. I asked how we were going with inserts for "A Week with God."

One of the producers piped up, "Jonas, I have some footage of this guy in Florida who believes the alligator in his backyard pond is God."

Everyone laughed but I returned the serve, "Well, Roger, how does he know the alligator is God? What proof does he have?"

The young producer looked up at me, "He says that when he recites the Lord's Prayer the gator goes to sleep." There was more laughter in the room.

I asked about other footage that I knew they had been assigned to shoot on the trip, "What about the video from the interview with Terry Jones?" Jones is the pastor of Dove World Outreach Center and wants to burn Qur'ans all the time.

Another producer spoke up, "He hasn't changed his tune. He feels the same way. The footage is a great example of how fundamentalism has poisoned some organized religious groups."

On a whiteboard behind us we had Monday to Friday mapped out in columns. I suggested, "Let's add that on Tuesday. Isn't that when we'll look at how people are persecuted for their beliefs?"

Everyone agreed and we keep filling things in for every day except Friday. For one of the nights we had booked a psychiatrist to talk about the long-term effect of repression, and how it makes some people do the exact opposite from what they are taught.

Then Roger tentatively raised his hand. I looked at him, "Yes, Roger?"

He took a drink of water then asked, "So, I heard you convinced the network to give you three hours on

Friday night. Ah, no disrespect here, Mr. Bronck, but why haven't we written any names on Friday?"

I looked at Gloria, and then said, "Well, we're trying to get a special guest and we want to make sure the time stays wide open."

Everyone in the room looked at each other with apprehension. I knew what they were thinking. We had always followed a creed on the show that was basically 'NO SECRETS – NO SURPRISES.' It appeared as if Gloria and I were keeping something from the team.

Just as the tension was ready to produce another question, Gloria stepped up, "Guys, right now the guest is top secret but it looks like we have a good shot at getting GOD for three hours."

The room was silent, and then major laughter erupted. Everyone seemed satisfied. Something that was so unbelievable seemed for a moment in time to be logically possible. I guess they all had faith in Gloria to produce the guest. Of course, with more than 75 percent of them believing there is a God, I guess everyone believed he should be a guest on God Week?

33.   The Fourth Encounter

On this rainy morning Gloria and I decided to share a cab. We also wanted to plot some strategy on how we would handle this fourth encounter. After greeting my companion on this incredible journey, I asked her, "Are you ready for this?"

She opened her iPad, sipped a hot coffee and answered, "Jonas, I have been up half the night. I have so many questions. I found this note, he said, 'I am the universe' and I wanted to ask him are there other gods who control other universes?"

I smiled at her. She always had a remarkable talent for finding the next best question to ask in any interview. I suggested, "No, let's get him into that position on the air, then we'll spring it on him."

Gloria chuckled, "Yea, catch the Big Guy with a trick question. Who are you - Dan Rather?"

Gloria scratched the question off her list and we continued through the New York City gridlock. The cab driver was eager to get us to our destination, zigging and zagging from avenue to street. Gloria looked at me, "I have a great idea. I have a stopwatch on my phone. Here's what I want to do. Just as we enter the room, I click the stopwatch on and then I'll stop it when we come out of the place. We can see the true duration of our conversation. This stopping time is some trick with our cell phones."

I agreed to the plan.

When we got to the building there was a woman with a French poodle in the doorway. I nodded a greeting, "Terrible day to walk the dog, huh?"

She smiled at me. "Yes, he is just going to have to hold it," she said.

I laughed and Gloria passed the doorman who was helping the woman back into the building. As we were going up on the elevator something hit me, "You know I've never seen anyone on the 13th floor."

Gloria thought for a second, "Yes, but then that could be just coincidence."

When we got to the door of 1313, I put the key into the lock, Gloria clicked the stopwatch and we went in. The two chairs were in the same place but the windows were open. The windows had never been open before. I walked over to close them and as I was closing them, we heard,

"I love the sound of rain; the water of life."

A bit startled, I ask, "You want them open?"

"Whatever you like," he returned.

After closing the windows, I got back to the chair next to Gloria. I was most curious of why the all-powerful Supreme Being had never greeted us, no "hello" or some other icebreaker common among mere mortals. The thought passed when Gloria started her aggressive tactics, "Let's go back to the beginning of the universe: The Big Bang. Why did this happen? What was your role?"

"Yes, are you the author?" I asked.

I could smell the rain in the room. The wind had changed and the wind was blowing in from the east. The rain was tapping on the windows.

"The Big Bang was the collapse of a black hole. This happens in the great infinite space every few hours. There are billions of them. New universes are being created as we speak."

I jumped in, "Let's go back to the beginning. We have this mass that contracts into a small center that has such great mass that it cannot be stable. It would be as if the whole Earth was reduced to the size of a golf ball. It would be so heavy it would defy comprehension, correct?"

"You seem to be a thinking journalist. Think of that great mass as the egg of life. No change can take place until it is penetrated by something. Just like sperm penetrating the human egg. At that moment, life begins. In the great infinite space, neutrinos passed through the mass and created the beginnings of this universe. It was an explosion beyond anything ever known to mankind."

Gloria entered the flow, "Did you send the neutrinos? Did you create the Big Bang?"

He spoke to us, **"Neutrinos are everywhere. Neutrinos are everywhere in the galaxy. They are in your sun. With every breath you take, tens of thousands of neutrinos pass through your body. The smartest human on your planet can't even determine their mass. They travel at near the speed of light and they can do so much**

more than your current knowledge allows you to understand."

"You didn't answer the question. What was your role in creating our universe?" I persisted.

He spoke with a softer tone, **"Yes, the neutrinos are God and God is the neutrino. They are everywhere and can be anywhere. Once the explosion was triggered, it began. All that happened after that is a natural process; a process that takes place in time infinite and in places near and far."**

Gloria jumped back in, "So, you are describing what some people would call the passive God. Like this guy Jake who asked this on the Internet: *You mean passive, like he knows everything that's going on but doesn't do anything about it, or passive as in totally unaware of what's going on?"*

I added, "I think she is asking about the big elephant in the room; creation or evolution?"

"There is clearly no elephant in the room but an elephant is a good example of evolution. You see the reason I want to go on TV is to straighten out some of your bad writers of the past and their creative imaginations that have hurt people. Disagreement starts small but then, like the universe, expands until your only resolution seems to be hate and killing."

Gloria looked up, "I am speechless."

I too, found myself being forced to decide again: Was this simply a plot to destroy our common Christian-Judeo-Islamic beliefs by some nefarious Dr. Evil with visual effects and voices coming from thin air? Or, were we getting somewhere, finally? I leaned forward, "So, evolution is real and not some intelligently designed set of different species?" Most religious skeptics would now ask God to prove if Darwin was on to something. A scientist would demand proof of what this force was saying. So, I asked, "What about the snowflake. Each one is unique. Many believers would say that is your proof of an intelligent designer. How can that be?"

"Oh really," God sounded amused. "That is their proof? How can anyone know if each flake is unique? Has anyone really looked at every snowflake under a microscope? Anyone who claims each of anything is totally unique needs to step up and prove they have actually observed millions of anything. A snowflake is just cold air, moisture and wind. You could make that in a wind tunnel."

Gloria leaned back confidently, "Why is it so hard for billions of people to understand evolution?"

God drew in a breath and began to speak as if he were explaining this concept for the hundred millionth time, "In five billion years things evolve. Why would any intelligent human being not see change as part of what your Earth is all about? Look at the Coywolf. Within the last 100 years, coyotes and wolves started to mate and created a new, hybrid animal. Evolution doesn't sit around waiting for you to figure it out. Look at your human bodies in the late 1800s and now look at how over-weight and out of shape people have become. That too, my children, is evolution."

I asked, "So you are defending mother nature?"

God spoke forcefully, **"Why do I have to defend nature? I am God."**

34.   The Connections

We are all connected. We are all part of the biology of the planet. Most experts say that 95 percent of our DNA is similar to the ape. And yet this science seems to get lost in the argument of evolution. The dogma of religious fervor attempts to blur the findings of biology and anthropology. Here I was sitting in a room talking to who many worship as the Supreme Being and I wasn't about to let a few major topics get overlooked.

I looked down at my black and white notebook and underlined one of my questions, "The religious leader Jerry Falwell said 'AIDS is not just God's punishment for homosexuals. It is God's punishment for the society that tolerates homosexuals.' Is that true?"

Gloria couldn't hold back, "And he also blamed the 9/11 attacks on pagans, abortionists, feminists, and the gays."

"In 2005, Mr. Falwell contracted a viral infection. Two years later he died of sudden cardiac death. Why did that happen? It happened because he was a sick man. He spent most of his life condemning people he didn't like or understand. Why would he die at 73 years of age? Why

would such an important messenger of God be taken from the world? Because he wasn't a prophet, he was just a man trying hard to shape the world in his own image."

Gloria continued with the line of questioning, "How does a person of faith know when someone is a true voice of the universe and not just someone blowing their own smoke?"

"I don't know about smoke, but no man has the right to judge another man or woman. When someone blames the innocent for things that happened because of terrorism or hate or natural law that man is a fool."

"There is some research that suggests that HIV was passed from chimpanzees to humans in West Africa," I continued, "Some think it was when people in Africa hunted and ate monkeys. Others think the disease was created by the production of polio vaccine that was cultivated in the living tissue of monkeys. What is man to do about viral infections?"

God spoke, **"Well, the first thing you have to do is to rethink your priority lists. AIDS is only the tip of the iceberg. You have MRSA and KPC and ebola and you** waste your money on holy wars and political brainwashing on TV. If you redirected the one trillion dollars you spent on the Middle East wars to focus on cures and science to deal with the inevitable spread of these viruses you would be doing something worthy. You feed your cattle, pigs and chickens antibiotics which then produces resistant strains of bacteria and viruses. You spend very little money on researching the effects of your actions. The people in power keep saying if it's good for business, then it's good for the world."

Gloria leaned in, "We were talking about evolution earlier. Isn't this just part of evolution? Some people might say this is just part of Darwin's view on survival of the fittest. It weeds out the weak from the herd."

"Yes, in a sense, there have been many plagues and threats that have fallen on the population of the Earth. Humans usually don't see the connections between the problem and their actions until it is too late. For example, the Romans found the metal lead very useful. They lined the aqueducts with lead and that came in contact with their drinking water. As the lead leached into the water supply, people suffered from lead poisoning. The severe cases caused seizures, coma, and death. Man causes most of the problems and by the time he finally realizes it, lots of people die. It's only then that the powers that be change things."

I was curious about this, "Is it simply due to the fact that we have too many people on the Earth? We can travel from anywhere on the planet in hours. We can spread a plague faster to more people than ever before."

"Earth is a big planet. You have room for a trillion people, but you have to start to figure out how to feed them and house them and protect them from evil viruses. If you had no countries and you just all worked together as one people, you could do so many great things for each other. Why do you let people in Africa eat bats and monkeys? You could do more globally without your religious walls."

Gloria looked down at her iPad and then slowly looked forward, "I almost think that the spread of these viruses is some kind of evolutionary acceleration. It seems clear to me that things that used to take millions of years to happen occur faster now with all our chemicals and pollution. But when people die within days of getting a viral infection, isn't that just the evil part of evolution?

"You are very bright, Gloria. Evolution is a round ball rolling down a hill. You just have to start it and it naturally keeps rolling. Evolution is not some square cube you have to keep turning to move. If you have a desire to survive, then you are certainly part of evolution. No human wants to die."

Gloria added, "No human wants to die unnecessarily."

35.   Morality

The rain stopped and the sun was bending around the clouds. The room was getting warm. I walked over and turned on the AC. Gloria made a few notes and when I sat back down, she was ready to take the conversation to the next level, "So, Lord, may I call you that? Where does morality come from? Did Charles Darwin really give us anything to go on there?"

"Why do you focus on Darwin?" God asked. "He was just doing his job and lots of people learned a lot from him. But he only dealt with things he could see. Let's look at the Earth and how it evolved. Yes, you might think the survival of the fittest was the first moral principle. If I eat you, I survive. If you eat me, I die."

I was fascinated by this, "Where does morality come from? If a survival mechanism can be said to be a kind of morality then where do those instincts come from?"

"Instinct is another one of the fine points of nature. The simple, innate, usually fixed pattern of

behavior in animals and humans in response to certain stimuli. The one I love most dearly is a parent's instinct to protect its offspring. That is connected to survival. If a parent didn't have this embedded desire to nurture and defend its most fragile chance at existence, where would that species be?"

Gloria jumped in, "How do we get this instinct? Did you teach us?"

"Gloria, there are no absolutes. Isn't that what science teaches you? But let's continue on this path. You asked where morality comes from and I say morality is your natural reaction. But you do know that there are some animals that eat their young: bears, hamsters and fish — must I go on? Is that wickedness or just hunger? "

I asked, "Are you saying what the fundamental Christians say, that God created all this beauty and life of the planet and that proves there is a God who loves us?"

"Let me put this in terms you can understand. No, beauty is not a survival of the fittest principal. A volcano erupting might be beautiful and powerful but if you live on that island without a boat you are doomed. Did God make the volcano kill the people because they were bad or did the fragile nature of the Earth's core randomly create the eruption? Nature doesn't have a reason when it creates an Earthquake, or floods the land or blows off the top of a mountain. It's just part of the process of the planet. But there has to be a gatekeeper of this universe. If another universe decided to drift into collision with your Earth they would win and you would be gone. I am protecting you from total annihilation."

Gloria fired back, "Do you have proof on that claim? Isn't that just chance, like anything else in the cosmos?"

"You can think of it that way but I would see it as the ultimate morality. I am not sure that people really understand enough yet to really grasp the concept. I am going to say a lot of things that will disturb and disrupt what humans think is true and right. I am going to disappoint a lot of people. And you, Mr. Bronck, will be held in contempt. You will be the victim of much abuse and ridicule. Are you ready for that?"

I thought about the question for a bit, "Well, this is more than a story. This is important. Maybe this can make a difference. What is the goal of all this, anyway? Peace on Earth, no wars, less hate, just maybe a little reciprocal altruism?"

Gloria quipped, "You sound like John Lennon!"

"Yes. Lennon, the musician. He said his band was *more popular than Jesus* and he was right. Why are we so concerned with what people say and write? There is a good reason. All belief and understanding comes from the recording of what has been told. Was there a God before there was the spoken or written word? Yes, but mankind did not know how to express the presence."

I saw an opening for a question, "Why did you let mankind spend so much time worshipping the sun, the planets or made-up deities, like Baal – the god of thunderstorms, fertility and agriculture?"

"This brings us to the question of free-will and the burden of believing that everything happens for a reason."

Gloria chimed in, "Yeah, that is what your mother says to you when something bad happens in your life. I could never figure out the reason behind bad things happening. What a misuse of the word: reason."

"You put your finger on it. Primitive man looked at the world in simple terms. If it didn't rain, he lost all his crops. No crops, no food. If the sun went dark during an eclipse, this was because mankind must have done something to make the gods angry. Rather daft don't you think?"

I offered, "We are primates; social animals as some say. We created agents whom we believed to be responsible for the bad things that happened. In our social consciousness, we thought we could bargain with that agent. Isn't that part of our makeup?"

Gloria followed up, "Fear has always been part of having a God? Fear and guilt seem to be connected to God, why is that?

"Man always felt he must please the god or gods so bad things didn't happen. People invented things they thought God wanted. Even as recent as the 1500s, Maya priests in the Yucatan peninsula sacrificed children by throwing them into sacred sinkhole caves to petition the gods for rain and fertile fields. As civilization advanced some people realized that killing members of your species was immoral. They created the religious movements.

They shifted to sheep being slaughtered on altars to please their gods. Somehow sacrifice is germane to organizing people into a religion."

I asked the final question of the morning, "Free will is part of evolution then? To get to the other side, both animals and man must exercise free will, even if they are wrong sometimes?"

There was a pause; then God spoke, **"Yes that is correct. Learning is part of evolution. The more man learns, the better he becomes at using his free will wisely. There are still many people in the world who decide to end their lives before their time is done. That is a use of free will. I deplore it. They don't realize that the next day might bring them all the answers to a better life. They take the chance of ending it one day too soon. And we go on."**

I asked with respect, "Yes, can we continue tomorrow; if it is your will."

"Yes, I've already determined, tomorrow is another day."

We got up and walked toward the door.

Gloria looked back and gave a slight wave. Once we got outside the door Gloria grabbed her phone and hit stop on the stopwatch. She looked at me as we walked to the elevator, "Oh my God, 13 seconds."

36.   True Friends

After we finished that night's show, Gloria made her way to my office and without thinking I asked her, "Hey, why don't you come over and we can get some order-in Chinese and talk."

The question didn't elicit any surprise, "Yeah, sure, we both have a lot to talk about." We loaded up our notes and devices and headed for the apartment.

One of the great things about Chinese food is no matter how much you order, you don't feel guilty because it always makes great leftovers the next day. After consuming large portions of Moo Shu chicken, I took the empty plates to the kitchen. I noticed two fortune cookies on the counter. I returned to my living room and poured Gloria another glass of red wine. I had my scotch.

"Jonas, you know this is either going to make or break us. And by break, I mean, get us tossed off TV forever."

I put my glass down on the table, "Yes, I know. Where are you on the 1 to 10 scale?

She smiled, "Well, I have to tell you, I am up at about 6 now. It was the damn stopwatch thing. It showed us the exact amount of time we were there. If it would have shown the actual duration we were there, I would have screamed this is a total fucking fraud! Let's get the hell away from this asshole."

I wondered why she would have this thought pattern, "I don't understand. Why would that result determine what you believe? It's just a number. Why do we rely more on our technologies and less and less on our guts?"

She curled up on the couch, "You don't see it? It's the 13th floor, apartment 1313 and the day you had lunch with Ida?"

I whispered, "I don't remember."

Gloria unraveled her legs, "It was Monday, the 13th and the Indian restaurant is at 13 Central Park South."

She had my total attention now, "What the hell? Why the number 13? That is usually a bad luck number."

Gloria added, "Case in point, Alex Rodriguez wore number 13."

We both laughed a bit and drank some more. I was getting tired but I wanted to talk about where we were going with this material. I leapt into the game, "On Friday the 13th in October 1307, King Philip IV of France ordered the arrest of the Knights Templar who were, well most of them, tortured and killed; back at you!"

Gloria was in, "Yes and then there is Apollo 13 launched at 13:13 central time, Houston is in the Central Time zone. But even though the mission was considered a total failure all the men got back and it made a great movie."

Then it was my turn, "There were 13 people at the Last Supper, 12 disciples plus Jesus. The 13th man, Judas, betrayed Christ."

Then Gloria, laughing now, "And there are 13 witches in a coven, while on the other hand, according to the Torah, God has 13 attributes of mercy. It's just a prime number."

The night wore on and we were getting no closer to figuring out what we were going to do with our personal God stashed in an apartment in Alphabet City. We were both a bit tipsy, but I wanted to ask one more question before the night got away, "Gloria, seriously now, why don't you believe in God?"

She took a large sip of wine, put the glass down and said, "I've always thought of religious people as 'anti-realists.' I see people who are so devoted to the Lord and

Christ and this whole dogma who really don't seem happy."

I suggested, "But there are also many devout Christians, Jews and Muslims who are very happy."

Gloria looked down to the floor, "I also see people who are overly happy about God. And I'm a little afraid of them. They spend all their waking hours thinking about God, or Jesus. See I have a problem with a belief system that seems to be creating more hurt than good."

"But I was asking you about God," I reminded her. "Not so much religion. I wasn't thinking about the Church, although, we'll have to ask God to explain that tomorrow."

Gloria nodded in agreement, "You see Jonas, I have always been taught by my parents that I'm smart and I'm equal to any man. And a lot of the stuff in religion tends to make a woman inferior or second class. I blame God for letting that happen, you know, if he exists."

I scratched my head, "So, our friend in the unlucky apartment #1313, does he seem blatantly chauvinistic or demeaning and misogynistic?"

Gloria thought, "Well, not yet. But we can only go on what we're taught and what we read. It all seems to be a battle between those who have no regard for science and evolution and those who think they know everything. I mean, I've read the great chauvinist Christopher Hitchens, the anti-delusionist Richard Dawkins and the skeptic Michael Shermer. It all makes sense but at the same time I think they are, excuse the pun, preaching to the choir."

I walked over and put my glass on the counter in the kitchen, "Do you have any guilt or regrets in your life?" I asked.

Gloria took the hint and brought her empty glass to the kitchen, "I know what is right and wrong. I don't need a Bible for that. I know that my parents love me. I know that you respect me. I get paid well and I only regret not making enough time to write a book."

I asked a personal question, "What about slowing down and having a family?"

She tried to get that last drop from the glass then said, "No, I don't have mommy guilt or some need to reproduce. I don't care about being married. I guess I'm not normal. I have never derived my happiness from another person or from a God. I love myself."

I leaned over and kissed her on her forehead, "Get some sleep, we have to talk to God tomorrow and I want you to be sharp. Take an aspirin before you go to bed to defeat the wine devil."

She grabbed one of the fortune cookies I had placed on the counter. She opened it and popped a piece of the cookie in her mouth. She read the fortune then laughed, "An old man will lead the way! That must be you, Jonas?"

I grimaced then opened the second cookie. I got real serious, "This one says, Toto pull the curtain back and expose the fraud of the wizard."

Gloria grabbed the fortune and quickly scanned it, "It doesn't say that!" We both laughed.

She gathered her computer bag and stuffed everything she was carrying in the small pouch on the side. There was something to be learned from all this and I was just hoping we could bring this whole thing to TV in a way that could do some good. I knew I couldn't do this without Gloria. She was such a strong, smart young woman.

She turned at the door, "You know I have to say one thing; I wish God was a late sleeper, this 8 o'clock crap is for the birds." The door closed.

37.   The Fifth Encounter

When I woke up, I felt lousy. My head hurt and my chest was tight. Was I getting a cold? It didn't matter, the task was at hand. There I was, an hour later, climbing into the elevator taking me to our fifth encounter. As we walked into the room, we heard our first greeting,

"Good morning Jonas, and good morning to you, Gloria. Are you feeling a little under the weather Mr. Bronck?"

Startled of course, I said, "Yes, I am. How did you —?" I stopped short.

Gloria was upbeat, "Good morning Mr. God, or is it Miss God? What gender are you? I assume with the male voice, you are male."

God spoke in a female voice, a rather perfect voice-over kind of female voice, `"Well, for you Gloria, let me use a different modulation."`

I commented to Gloria, "I hope that makes you feel better."

Then we heard, `"And now you feel better as well, Jonas."` As remarkable as everything about this thing had been, there was something more than special this day.

Just at that moment, I felt much better. I wondered if I should thank God, so I did, "Thanks, God." I felt like a modern day Lazarus.

Gloria sat down, brought out all her notes and launched right into the day, "Okay, you knew we would get to this and certainly all our viewers have a vested interest in the next topic: religion. When does the awareness of God begin, with Noah or Moses? What are we going to say about the Bible?"

God in female voice spoke, "The Epic of Gilgamesh written in Mesopotamia around 2,500 years before the birth of Jesus contains a flood story almost exactly the same as the Noah account in the Bible. So, if you want to work from known, written accounts, we can do that, but I have to warn you what you are about to hear might be rather disturbing to the devout in your audience."

I leaned forward, "What about this whole experience isn't Earth shattering?"

God spoke again, "Are you being patronizing or do you really believe that?"

Gloria came to my rescue, "I gotta say the male voice thing worked better for me. The female avatar seems a bit on edge." The voice returned to the deep male voice,

"Okay, as you wish. So you think the male approach would be better on TV?"

I couldn't believe we were talking to God about what voice the Almighty should use on cable TV. I suggested, "Well, most people believe you are male. They always refer to God as a male, they use 'he' or 'him' when referring to you."

"Yes, this is the greatest challenge. From the beginning of time, men were the hunters. They were strong and got stronger. They ate more food; they needed muscles to survive. They always got the lion's share of meat. While women had to focus on food cultivation, preparation and, of course, care of the offspring. It was the pecking order of the centuries."

Gloria offered, "I don't understand why the women weren't part of the storytelling, the creators of the myths, and eventually the writing of those myths."

God continued, **"They were. But their stories and rhymes and songs were to entertain the children. Their little games, like peek-a-boo, weren't told around the camp fire late at night. The poetry of women was not the epic stories of sneaking up on a beast in the forest and bringing him to his knees."**

I ventured, "The story about Noah was probably an old folk tale that never really happened?"

"Well floods happened and villages were wiped out and people lost their lives but the idea that somehow Noah was saving all the animals of the world and a few God-fearing people just didn't happen."

Gloria's eyes opened wide, "What I found so unbelievable was that Noah was 480 when they say you asked him to build a boat. He survives the flood and then

350 years later he dies at the age of 950 but then the Bible downgrades his lifespan from 1,000 years to 120 years. What was that all about? Or was time measured differently?"

"I never asked him to build an ark. It's a myth. Yes the Bible starts out with a myth that is no different than that of Deucalion, the son of Prometheus and Pronoia in Greek mythology. He was warned of a great flood by Zeus and Poseidon; so he builds an ark and stuffed it with creatures. After the flood, he is given advice from the gods on how to repopulate the Earth. Deucalion also sends a pigeon to find out the condition of the world and the bird returns with an olive branch."

"What man would need instruction on how to populate the Earth?" Gloria asked.

I shook my head in disapproval and continued, "Yes of course, I learned that in the Joseph Campbell mythology course I took. But then why do theologians and apologists deny the connection to earlier myths?"

Gloria asked, "Why do people keep doing Sherlock Holmes over and over?"

"You will have to ask them. But one of the things we have to realize is that man has this need to claim ideas. They use ideas to get their point of view across, or worse, control other people. Eight thousand years before the birth of Jesus there were 5 million people on the Earth. Surprise? And by the time we have the Moses story etched into history there were 10 million people living on the planet. They were all over the place but most of them didn't read or write."

"What's your point?" asked Gloria.

"What I am trying to point out is the lack of logic. Yes the Israelites were leaving Egypt after being enslaved for some say 250 years, while some say 400 years. Don't know why they wouldn't have remembered the exact number of years? When Moses goes up to pray on the

mountain, he stays there for 40 days without much water or food. Imagine what he thought he saw after not eating for days. They are called hallucinations."

Gloria added, "No one has ever found any artifacts or proof that the Jewish people were even in Egypt at that time. With all the digging by archeologists you'd think they would have found something?"

I had to interrupt, "Are saying that you did not talk to Moses through a burning bush?"

God continued, **"He saw the burning bush; I know nothing of it. According to the Bible, Moses came down from the mountain with the Ten Commandments. Why out of the ten million people in the world would I have only given these important commandments to one person? If I was going to drop the laws and absolute rules on the people of the world I would have done a much wider distribution."**

Gloria asked, "So what is the Bible?

"It was the work of many writers over a period of 100 years trying to write some kind of historical document. It's an interpretive work not a legal document. It's a mix of myth, misinformation and manipulation. It is the work of a driven committee to please God, the way the committee saw it. Those who thought they were smarter than everyone else delivered a doctrine to those without the power of the pen or intellect. There was no disagreement or questioning."

I had to ask, "That means Moses is a myth?"

"They say that Moses came down from the mountain with his big old tablets of rules, which he wrote himself and I punished the Jews for breaking rules they didn't know they had yet? And then, if I was the forgiving Lord of the New Testament, why would I make them wander in the desert for 40 years. Their 'promised' land wasn't that far away. What an unnecessary burden on people who were just freed from slavery. Is he a myth? Well, most of what they wrote is a myth, based on a leader who obviously didn't know much about geography."

I took a deep breath, "I think Gloria and I need a little break here. It's time to take a walk around the block, if you don't mind."

As Gloria got up she said, "We promise it won't be 40 years."

38.   Out with the Old

As we walked down Avenue D, the sun was hitting the pavement. The heat came up from the concrete. I looked at my cell phone. It was 8:05 a.m. We were out of the timeless mode and moving north. I looked at Gloria and broke the silence, "What are you thinking?"

Gloria took a quick look at her phone, "Well, I don't think anyone will think this is real when it's on TV. I think they'll laugh at us. This could kill the network. Sponsors will take a bunch of heat from the Christian right. I cannot even believe there is a 'right' part of a religion. I thought that was for political parties."

We walked across the street at the light and then turned back toward the apartment. I looked up at the tall buildings, "Well, we have gone this far and I do have to admit I am very curious about where this is going."

Gloria agreed, "I'm with you captain, my captain."

I looked at her as the sad facts of Robin Williams' death surfaced in my mind, "Let's go back."

We got back to the apartment but oddly enough, the doorman stopped us and asked who we wanted to see. I held up the key showing him 1313 with the logo of the building on it. He said, "Oh boy, that's the original key ring, that's an antique. Go on up."

When we got into the elevator, I said, "That was strange. I wonder what changed about us."

"Maybe we're getting closer to God." Gloria offered.

A few minutes later, we were back to our positions and ready for round two. I began, "So the Ten Commandments, you had nothing to do with them?" We waited for quite a while. It was like something was wrong. Like maybe the pranksters weren't ready for our return. Just at the point when I was going to say something, he broke his silence,

"Did you work out all your emotional reactions to the truth?"

"We just needed a break. It was getting a bit intense in here. Hey, we're just humans." Gloria grinned.

"Getting back to the Commandments; Yes, I guess I have a problem with people who make things up. What do you think of the Ten Commandments?"

Remembering a show we did on the commandments, I answered, "Well, I get what Moses was trying to do. I've always liked 'Honor thy mother and father,' 'Thou shall not kill,' 'Thou shall not steal,' not sure about some of the others."

"I would never say the words 'I am a jealous God'. You cannot have it both ways. You cannot say that I am all powerful, omnipotent, omnipresent and in charge of everything and then say that I am jealous. That is a human fault and I am not human. I am a force beyond humanity."

Gloria said, "Okay, so you are okay with the graven images of anything that is in heaven?"

I added, "And the part about someone who takes your name in vain?"

"Why would I care if someone used a curse like 'God damn you' for another person? They have no power

over the universe. Maybe the person deserves to be talked to in that manner?"

Gloria asked, "Here's a bigger question for you. With all these commandments and laws, they don't seem to do any good. They haven't stopped people from sinning. What does God say about that?"

"Those are the laws of men. Men who had the right idea but they couldn't stop there. The more men huddled in dark rooms with their self-proclaimed power over other people, the further their doctrine moved away from the goals of Godly goodness. They merged poor historical records with home-brewed morality and rules to keep the people in line. Their views were important because they said they were."

I needed a clarification, "You mean the high priests of ancient Israel?"

"Yes, they were trying to keep the peace and keep their people healthy and happy but they had to keep making laws. It is the same today. You just keep making laws. Most people don't really read the Bible, they just quote a few sayings, and read along with the church-goers on Sunday but they don't take the time to see how vindictive, jealous and heavy-handed they made me out to be in the Old Testament."

Gloria extended the line of thinking, "You mean like the book of Leviticus?"

He continued, "Yes, pages and pages of instructions on how to slaughter a goat in the temple. Why would God want them to kill an animal on the altar in the temple and touch the blood with their fingers? And they created a list of what to eat and not eat. They said not to eat the meat of any animal that has cleaved hoof or those that chew their cud. So they didn't eat camels, but they cooked and ate antelope and goat. They didn't even know which ones chewed their cud."

I asked, "What about the rules on women and childbirth?"

"A woman couldn't come to the sanctuary for 33 days after having a baby because she needed to be purified. Why would they say that? What is impure about having a baby?"

Gloria said, "They really didn't think that much of women. They said a man is worth 50 shekels of silver in temple tax, whereas you only have to pay 30 shekels for a woman. By law, we were never equal."

"And they talk about these complicated rules on owning and redeeming a slave. The holy Bible sanctioned slavery."

Gloria kept going, "And what about the sex lives of the citizens?"

God continued, **"The rules say that man can sleep with a slave girl but if you sleep with your daughter in-law both of you will be killed. If a man lies with another man both will be put to death; rather homophobic. If a man sleeps with his wife and his mother-in-law all three will be put to death. If you sleep with an animal, you will be put to death. Did they really even have to say that? If a man has sex with his wife while she has her period both will be sent away."**

Gloria said, "Tribes were known to kill misshaped babies and even people who were considered a biological threat."

"Yes and people they called dwarfs, or those maimed, lame or with blemishes were not welcome in the temple. If you blaspheme the Lord you will be put to death by stoning. And people wonder why this still happens in the Middle East. It's in the Bible."

Gloria smiled, "So the Old Testament is out?"

I suggested, "But isn't it just all allegory today?"

"When the result of a rule means people are put to death for breaking unreasonable laws what we have is not symbolism, or a parable or a metaphor; it's a serious injustice."

I asked, "Are you offended by these rules?"

"What I am most offended by is the suggestion that when one person would break a law or commandment that I would inflict pain on third and fourth generations of those who offended me. Why would a loving God who wants mankind to live in peace and tranquility think like a terrorist? I am not a terrorist, I am God."

39.   Messiah Time

The planets certainly aligned on this day. The network pre-empted our show for midterm election coverage so I got the night off. Gloria wanted to work but I sent her home. The last couple of weeks had been fatiguing on both physical and mental levels. This was the perfect time for me to have dinner with one of my favorite friends, Reverend and Doctor Samantha Smith. Sam is on the faculty of the Union Seminary in New York and we had actually planned this dinner a few months ago. I not only wanted to see if she could be a panelist on "A Week with God" but I also wanted to pick her brain about a theory I had about how all this got started.

We met at a French bistro on the Upper West Side, "Hi there Sam, how have you been?" I hugged her and sat down, "Did you check your schedule? Can you make it for our God Week?"

She smiled from ear to ear, "Well, my husband is teaching in Ireland all month so I am all yours."

I replied, "Okay, that's great. I'll have Gloria call you and set up the day. You know we have to pay you at least the union minimum?"

She laughed, "That is fine, I work at Union, union is good."

I got serious, "The planning for this week has really taken me places I never thought I would go, emotionally and physically."

"Yes, the Lord will work you hard, especially when you challenge him." Sam added.

I joked, "So, he is a man?"

Sam returned, "Well, when he does dumb things he is."

We both laughed and ordered our food. During our meal, I directed the conversation to the subject on my mind, "Tell me about prophesy, what is that all about?"

Dr. Smith explained, "Well, pretty simple, really. It's the process where a message is given from God to a prophet, who then communicates it to others. The Divine Source is, in a sense, using prophets as conduits to help people here on Earth know the future."

I queried, "The coming of the Messiah was very important to the Jewish people?"

Sam continued, "Yes, they called it an emanation, which is the origination of the world by a series of hierarchically descending radiations from the Godhead through intermediate stages to matter."

I leaned in, "Whoa, you lost me there. What does that mean?"

Sam continued, "Well, it's not that complicated, let's take Jesus. The Old Testament has 44 prophecies that predicted and were fulfilled by Jesus, thus the belief that he was the Messiah. Someone else claims 61 but let's stick to the Old Testament."

I chimed in, "But the Jewish authorities never agreed that he was the Messiah. Why would they not agree when 44 points of proof were cited from the basis of their own religion?"

Sam looked at her cappuccino, stirred the foamy drink then said, "Well, that is not what the Jews believe. And you must hear their side of the story. The Messiah was to build the Third Temple, gather all Jews back to the Land of Israel, usher in an era of world peace and end all hatred, oppression, suffering and disease. But that's not all; God would have become the King over the entire world. God would be *One* and His Name would be *One*. The historical fact was that Jesus fulfilled none of these messianic prophecies."

"That's a pretty tall order." I commented.

Sam smiled, "This wasn't picking what kind of car to buy. This was the coming of the Messiah."

"Different rules I guess," I reflected. "This was far from our expression, a self-fulfilling prophecy. Didn't the Jewish elders see those were impossible prophecies to achieve?"

Sam smiled, "Hey I didn't write it. I'm just reporting it."

I wanted to take this further, "It's amazing they combined the new and old testaments into one Bible. They were both using the books as proof for their point of view?"

Sam responded, "There are many points of disagreement, mostly on Mary's virginity. The Bible says it was a virgin birth. The Qur'an claims a virgin birth of Jesus while the Jews do not believe that."

I asked, "Isn't that important in the determination of whether Jesus was the Messiah?"

Sam replied, "Yes, it was important that the real Messiah of the Jewish people be the descendant of King David. Without a father how could Jesus have any relation to King David?"

I questioned, "Isn't God the father of King David in a way?"

She added, "There is a real Catch-22 in the verse in Isaiah 7:14 when it describes Mary as an *alma*. That word has always meant *a young woman*. We believe Mary was probably around 14 or 15 years old. Here is your smoking gun, Mr. Bronck. Christian theologians changed the word to *virgin*. The virgin factor made it special to the first century pagans who loved the idea of mortals being impregnated by gods."

I sat back, "It was a recruitment tactic in a sense."

Sam smiled, "I don't think they were thinking that far in advance, just short-term conversions."

I tapped on the table, "Every time I get together with you I learn so much. Man, something that happened more than 2,000 years ago and we're still debating the finer points of one book. Let me ask you this: Do you think Jesus was a real person or just a myth?"

Sam smiled brightly, "Absolutely he was a real person. He walked on the Earth and was a wise and important teacher; sources confirm that he lived. Even the Romano-Israel scholar and historian Titus Flavius Josephus, also known by his Jewish name, Joseph ben

Matityahu, wrote a very compelling history of the Jewish people called *Antiquities of the Jews.*"

I said, "Yes, I've seen that work; hard to read in that strange construct of English."

Sam continued, "He was a defector in one of the wars and ended up on the Roman side of things. In his book, he talks about Jesus' brother James being put to death by the Romans. Although some scholars believe there may have been some forgery by Christians who handled the creative translations."

"Is he the son of God?" I asked.

Sam smiled again, "He has to be, or all the Christian religions fall apart."

As I walked toward my apartment that night, I couldn't help but notice the large metal gates protecting the big red doors of the neighborhood church. Lying on the top step, leaning against the security gate on a cardboard box was a homeless man. I shook my head and wondered what would God think about the church keeping the neediest people out at night? Maybe I'll ask him.

40.   The Sixth Encounter

For some reason, I awoke with all the vim and vigor of a young man in college ready for the quest of knowledge. The experience of getting to know God in this strange interviewing process has given me this connection with the past, the present, and dare I say, excitement about the future.

As Gloria and I entered the lobby of the Qenatas Arms, we both noticed the devilish grin on the face of the doorman as we walked toward the elevator. As we got into the elevator, I commented, "I wonder what he had for breakfast?"

When the elevator door closed, Gloria blurted out, "Jeez, that asshole thinks we're having an affair."

I looked at her with surprise, "What are you talking about?"

She laughed, "Don't you get it? We come here together every morning at the same time. We go up, but remember we're in the land of frozen time. When we come back down in a few minutes and we leave. What else could that be?"

I considered her angle and responded, "That's embarrassing."

She laughed again, "You think? But really Jonas, it's much more embarrassing for you. From his vantage point, we're only up there for a few minutes; now that's a quickie." She winked, I blushed.

Sitting in the chairs like the king and queen, we were ready for the sixth encounter with God. I began with a question, "I have been thinking about how we just threw out centuries of history with the Old Testament. Why would those writings, documents and prophecies all be so easily disregarded by you?"

"The Bible is an incredible work. It was a document of many people who were trying hard to chart a path for primitive people. People who believed the Earth was a flat pancake of land and the sun and stars rotated around it as if a scenery designer had created it. When the researchers and thinkers revealed that the Earth wasn't flat pancake with a revolving sun, the high priests worked to silence - either by jail or death."

Gloria cleared her throat, "I have always wondered about the original sin. What was that all about? Adam and Eve were in paradise. I assume that was Africa, and everything was going so peachy. Then Eve just wants to eat some fruit and this snake, I assume the Devil, encourages her to put some fiber in her diet and WHAMMO the two of them get thrown out of the garden?"

"That was just another myth to explain why life on the Earth seemed so aimless and difficult. At the time of Jesus' birth, only 50 percent of all the babies born survived. With half of your offspring dying and endless wandering around in search of food and water, life wasn't so great. It started out with basic rules. Remember for every discovery of what mushroom in the forest was poisonous there was a dead body. The leaders wanted to make sure someone didn't eat the wrong thing and die. So they used the fear tactic. They proclaimed that if you ate

the wrong food you would go to hell. Ancient man used fear and guilt all the time."

I made a note and pushed forward, "A sin is defined as an act of violating God's will or a diversion from the ideal order of human beings. Where does sin come from?"

Gloria added, "Yeah, how come all the rules seemed to benefit man and make his life better?"

God paused, then answered, "**The smart thinkers of early man observed things in nature and used those to help form his philosophical credos. A moth flies around the room then dives into the flame and dies. Attracted by the light he commits the ultimate sin. He kills himself. Man thought, I have to explain to those who don't understand the dangers out there what is right and safe. And what could bring harm to that man and perhaps the whole tribe. It's just too bad that whole Garden of Eden story put all the blame on the female character.**"

Gloria jumped in, "But might not the flame also be a metaphor for religion and zealous belief. Yes, the light is bright but once you fly into the hot flame you lose yourself?"

God continued, **"You are very bright and clever, like a man from Bethlehem."**

I thumbed through my notes from my dinner with Dr. Smith, "Yes, tell us please, why the Jews were obsessed with a coming Messiah? As a matter of fact, there are 44 prophecies in the Old Testament that kept referencing who the Messiah would be. What was that all about?"

"If we must return to ancient text, yes, there are polarizing forces at work here. As I explained before, there are things that pull and things that push. The people of the tribe of Judah, or some say the Kingdom of Judah, which began about 1,000 years before the birth of Jesus, had a very rough time. These people had to fight constantly to keep their kingdom on this Earth. Between being taken as slaves by the Egyptians, then the

Babylonians, they prayed to God constantly to save them from bondage. They created the Messiah myth to give people hope. As in an action movie, one day the hero will come and defeat those who oppress us. Remember the scripture told them to take the land of Canaan and kill all the men, women and children who lived there. That sounds a bit more than an eye for an eye."

Gloria said, "They believed that a Messiah would come and free them."

I added, "The thing I learned last night was the qualifier for the Jewish leaders was this notion of not only freeing the Jews from all slavery but delivering world peace, ending all hatred, oppression, suffering and disease. They made the Messiah sound like God on Earth."

God's voice now was stoic and unemotional, **"Yes, they wanted it so much. They kept praying and even when some thought a man fit the bill, they couldn't see him as** the Messiah. It's remarkable that the Jewish people never found their man."

Gloria chimed in, "You're God, why didn't you give them a champion?"

God continued, **"Mankind has a strong desire to chart its own course. And when man sets his mind on some goal he will do anything to get there. Sometimes humans want things so badly that they will blindly find something or someone that fits their preconceived vision of things, like Jesus. Slavery was the Jewish nemesis, yet they did nothing to suppress it in their own laws. Free will has its drawbacks."**

Gloria was at the edge of her chair, "Let's get to the big question on the table, was he your son, was he the Messiah?"

41.   The Son of Man

There are moments in your life that you never forget: your first kiss, your first sexual experience, your first child, the death of a loved one and hopefully, you are aware during your own death, assuming there is a heaven. The idea of living forever and the nature of the human soul are the questions that seem unanswerable, yet extremely intriguing. Are we a body and soul or just a body? Can we ever find an objective reality? We're taught by science that absolutes are very difficult to attain. We haven't been able to achieve absolute zero in temperature, but we've close. We're taught that we can never travel at the speed of light. We're taught many things, but we still have the power to question what we're taught.

They tell us there are more than 2.18 billion Christians in the world. Nearly a third of the soon to be 7 billion people on this Earth believe that a man born of a virgin in Bethlehem was the Messiah, the son of God. Now we had a chance to talk to God and know the truth. I wanted this to be the focal point of our TV interview and the big payoff. I was focused and wanted to ask my big question, "God, tell us about Jesus."

"Jesus was a remarkable young man. Yes, he did exist and he did walk the Earth. To put this in perspective, we have to go back to the beginning. What I am about to reveal might change the way the people of this planet think and act for some time."

"We understand the magnitude of it," Gloria said.

God continued, "The Jewish laws were strict and unforgiving. There was a man who was a laborer, who toiled with stone masonry and wood but mostly stone. His name was Joseph. He was a hard-working, honest man who believed in the rabbis and the power of the temple. You might say he was a simple man."

I interrupted, "He wasn't a carpenter?"

"There really wasn't much wood in that part of the country. Most of the wood was used to make fishermen's boats or to construct furniture for the wealthy. Most of the work that Joseph and Jesus did was with stone. People slept on the stone floor on goat-hide mattresses filled with straw."

Gloria suggested, "Not a carpenter, but a mason. Who knew?"

"You see Joseph met a young woman. She was around 14 years of age. This strong, beautiful soul seemed like an angel sent to Joseph. She was young and naïve about the ways of men. When she was in the field picking flowers a Roman soldier came to her and asked her what she was doing. She told him she was just picking flowers. He forced her to the ground and, as she would tell Joseph, he laid on me and made me hurt."

Gloria mouthed, "Oh my G, G, God; that was Mary."

"Yes, and Joseph knew that if she was pregnant out of wedlock she would be stoned to death. Joseph also feared that if the high priests thought he was the father he too would be put to death. It was an easy choice to make. As soon as Mary appeared to be with child they left town and headed for a friend's home near Bethlehem. It was early June when they arrived there and Joseph declared to his friends that Mary was his wife."

I jumped in, "What about the prophecy? What about the virgin birth?"

"Without newspapers and TV and the Internet, the people of the world at that time passed stories along. Myths grew bigger than the person. All people have this tendency to slightly embellish a story as it passes from person to person. They wanted a Messiah and they heard a rumor that Joseph was not the father. They also heard the rumor that this might be a virgin birth. Think about all the religions and myths where some deity impregnates a human woman as the only path to deliver a man-god to the Earth."

Gloria added, "Even the Ancient Alien people believe extraterrestrials came here to impregnate human women."

"So, you aren't the father?" I asked.

God got more forceful, **"If I wanted to put a Messiah on the Earth I would just put him or her there. Why would I wait for a kid to grow up? If the world needed to be saved I wouldn't make the population of the world wait 33 years to be saved."**

"So, tell us more about his story," I suggested.

"He was a fairly normal kid and very bright. He wanted to know as much about Jewish scripture as possible. Even though he was from a lower-class background, he seemed to think of himself as someone special. Mary helped him with his self-confidence. He

saw his mother and many go without. He kept questioning why some people had wealth and food at the ready while others had to scratch out a living for a morsel of nourishment."

"The Romans, you know the bad guys, did they really go to Bethlehem and kill all the male babies?" Gloria asked.

"Another myth created by the writers. The idea that the Maji, the three wise men, would have visited the birth of Jesus and told King Herod that a new King of the Jews was born in Bethlehem is a bit of a stretch. First of all, no one knew Joseph and Mary and they weren't in a stable. They were in the basement of a friend's house. Yes, they kept their sheep in the basement at night but this was the only place in the house where they could have some privacy while she delivered the baby. But I would be remiss if I didn't mention that King Herod was a truly evil paranoid person who killed lots of people, including his wife and two sons."

I leaned forward, "Why did Jesus begin to teach and preach?"

God became calm, **"Jesus was quite impressed with people who saw things his way. He kept asking the high priests if he could get involved in the practice of sacrificing at the temple. They rebuked him several times. This made him feel like he was a second class citizen even in his own temple."**

Gloria jumped in, "So this inferiority complex drove him to a closer relationship with you. Did you tell him that everything was going to be okay and that he would be part of the holy trinity someday?

"I never talked to him. I listened."

42.　　Salty Water

I looked at Gloria and saw a woman fully focused and absorbed in what she was hearing. I admired her tenacity and depth. I knew that this was an intellectual pursuit for her, while for me; it was more as if my emotional base was being eroded away. Perhaps the teachings of the church had created a need for a savior in my life. I remember the first time I learned about the birds and the bees – why do we even use that euphemism? I was on the street catching baseball with my friends when one of the older boys said, "You know how you make babies, right?" Up to this point I thought that you just had to kiss real hard. When the older lad blurted out something about penises and vaginas, I was shocked. I'm embarrassed to admit my comeback was, "My parents wouldn't do that." I'm sure glad they did, if not, I wouldn't be here. But now it was the time to get, as the famous radio announcer would say, to the rest of the story.

Gloria checked something off her notes, "What was the turning point for Jesus of Nazareth? When did he start to believe that he had a calling?"

"The writers of the Bible seem to be missing a lot of details of Jesus' life between the age of 18 and late 20s.

This is when he broke away from his parents and started to find ways of making money so he could eat. It was when he heard about a man named John the Baptist that things changed for him. Yo anan, as John the Baptist was called, had this notion that the high priests of the temple were blocking, or at least filtering, the people's access to God. I agreed with John. And rather than intervene, I was curious to see how the authorities would react to his actions."

Gloria seized the moment, "You do have the power to change things? Why do people have to die in order for things to be played out?"

God increased the volume, **"Man has to find his own way while I keep the planets from slamming into each other."**

I had to interject, "Please tell us more. What was John the Baptist's role with Jesus?"

"John was convinced that all people had to do was be dunked in the water, a prayer said for them and they would be forgiven."

Gloria asked, "Of the original sin?"

"No, not at all. The whole concept of 'original sin' wasn't introduced until 200 years after Jesus by Irenaeus, the Bishop of Lyons. John the Baptist was just adapting the mikvah, a ritual immersion bath, part of Jewish life for generations. It was a symbolic, spiritualistic cleansing. Men did it every week and women did it right after their periods. John the Baptist found a river with deep enough water right on the border. The Roman soldiers watched him from their horses on the west bank and they reported back to Herod."

"The baptism made them feel more spiritual and closer to God. They didn't get that at the temple." I suggested.

"More and more people came. Jesus was impressed with how he felt after he was baptized himself. He wanted to learn how to baptize people. John liked Jesus and enjoyed the attention his young disciple gave him. Jesus hung on John's every word. And as he saw how many poor people came to the river, and how they left with smiling faces Jesus decided that this was his calling."

Gloria asked, "Is that when he started to say he was the son of God?"

"He never said that. He never said he was the King of the Jews. He never thought of himself that way, but when John had a dream of his own demise and Jesus appeared in his dream with this glow around his whole body that changed everything for Jesus."

I pushed back, "It was only a dream?"

"Yes, so John the Baptist was very persuasive and had Jesus very much in his hand. He told Jesus that he was the Messiah and that he should spread the word. People didn't need a church or temple to talk to God. They could talk to God whenever they wanted, directly. John was doing two things: making sure his legacy of baptism, 'his' great idea, would prosper, but also that Jesus would be motivated to continue to work against the religious leaders of day. If you say something enough to someone they start to believe it."

Gloria interjected, "Yeah, like Johnnie Cochran telling O.J. he didn't kill his wife until voilà, O.J. believed it."

"O.J. did kill his wife but you didn't need me to tell you that."

I got us back on track, "So what happened to John must have affected Jesus greatly."

"Yes, King Herod got worried when more and more people joined John the Baptist. The Roman soldiers believed that some kind of armed rebellion wasn't far off. As the crowds grew, so did Herod's fear of what was happening in the river."

Gloria said, "Something bad was about to happen."

"Yes they arrested him. During the celebration of his daughter's birthday, a drunken Herod promised that he would give her whatever she wanted. When the child asked her mother what on Earth should she ask for, the mother, who was playing Herod like a fiddle, suggested that her little girl ask for the head of John the Baptist on a platter. Some say Herod was repulsed by the idea but don't let those historians fool you. As I said he was an evil man. He cut John the Baptist's head off."

Gloria piped in, "Oh, boy, that is bad."

"And the effect on Jesus?" I asked.

"Jesus cried. He cried for a long time. John was like a father to him. John was his savior. He kept praying and praying asking for a message from above. I knew Jesus would work it out. I knew he would be able to overcome this terrible calamity."

Gloria responded, "You left Jesus out to dry?"

"It taught him that a belief system always has a political implication, as it does today. Jesus was determined to walk the Earth and tell everyone about truth and love and honesty. He planted the seed in all men and women that they are equal under God. And they are."

I asked, "Why did they use the term 'king' when they knew that would irritate the powers that be?"

"Jesus misused a metaphor for what some would call a kingdom on Earth with no castles, no walls and no

armies. Probably not the best choice of words, but he was human."

I suggested, "But the kingdom on Earth wasn't the main uplifting philosophy of Jesus."

God continued, **"The early Christians had a powerful message. It was the golden rule:** *Do to others what you want them to do to you.* **Sure, Jesus was an optimist. That is why he added the suggestion that people should love their enemies. He was trying to keep the peace. He wanted to avoid violence. Of course, he didn't comprehend that his enemies would eventually kill him. He truly believed he would live forever, like John the Baptist told him."**

I asked the question again, "Let me see if I got this right; Jesus wasn't the son of God?"

"He was the son of man, as he said. He was a poet and a man of high moral quality and kindness. He always

said he knew not his real father so every man was his father."

Gloria suggested, "It sounds like he had real daddy issues?"

"If you don't know who your father is, you have to love everyone. Even one of his enemies might have been his real father. Herod might have even been his father. Jesus was the son of man out to free all men and women from the fears instilled in them from the beginning of myth creation. He didn't see a purpose for the few powerful men in the Temple to dictate the relationship one had with God. He was a great man with high ideals and dreams. He would struggle greatly knowing that the symbol of his teachings today is the cross. The place he suffered so is now a golden piece of jewelry. Man is not always thoughtful and most of the time, he is just self-serving."

43.   Back to Life

Ironically I found myself back at the Indian restaurant where Ida Pearlstein had summoned me for the opportunity of a lifetime. This time I was at the same table with another old friend, Steve Summerville. "What's the news from Minnesota, Steve?"

Summerville was starting to show some signs of the menace that was growing throughout his body. His face was the color of ash. His hands trembled as he reached for the naan bread. My old friend was up against a villain much greater than he, "Well, Jonas, I am fine. Just more damn tests. I am sick of all these tests," he said as he stuffed his mouth with the bread.

"What about the bone marrow from your son?" I asked.

There seemed to be a hush in the restaurant at that moment. Steve lowered his voice, "He said he would do it but there is something strange about his DNA."

I put my fork down, "What does that mean?"

I could see a look of embarrassment, "Well, mystery solved, as they say on TV. They don't think he's my son."

I didn't know what to say, this was highly personal information coming from my boss, and I felt unable to answer. I tried to move on, "But can't there be another donor?"

He swallowed the bread, then in a stronger voice, "Forget about that shit, let's talk some business. Where are you with this "God Week" or whatever you are calling it? Do we have that special guest lined-up?"

I smiled, "Well yes, I think we do, but I am not sure you are going to like it. He really doesn't have a form, just a voice. We thought, well, he thinks that it would be kind of misleading if we had him sit there like a hologram or an Avatar."

Steve looked angry, "What the hell are you talking about? If he's God he ought to just come out of the closet and be himself. Ah, it is a HE, right?"

I chuckled, "Okay, I will ask him to do that but how do you want to handle how we promote this?"

Steve loved to be involved in promos for shows. He had a knack for coming up with these great catch phrases, "Why don't we go with a rundown of all the people who are going to be guests for the week, and we have the days of the week, you know, flying over the screen. Then we get to Friday and we have a big question mark. And the announcer says: you won't believe who is coming to TNN on Friday... the real expert on God."

I nodded in agreement the way we all do when the boss is speaking then posed, "But how do we handle the press? They are going to want to know who the guest is. They'll see that we have three hours slotted out for one guest. The advertisers and agencies will want to know what is going on as well."

Steve became more animated, "Screw the advertisers, we'll have no commercials!"

My jaw dropped, "Really, three hours, no commercials? That would be amazing. That will certainly make everyone think it's going to be the Pope or something."

Steve smiled, "Yes, this is great TV. We'll kill Fox."

After lunch, I walked back to the office. Along the way I passed group of young Muslim girls with their heads covered. I thought about God and what he would say about a rule that said that women had to cover their faces and bodies or men had to wear hats in holy places. What is it with religion and head covers?

As I entered my office, I saw a piece of paper on my desk. It was a note from Dr. Samantha Smith. She thanked me for the dinner, but the last line of the letter was strange. The sentence was short but potent: *Things aren't what they appear to be.* I thought that was an odd way to end a letter. She did sign the letter — *Peace in Christ* — which was more her style.

I didn't have time for that now. Gloria was in my office and she was in a panic. I looked at her and then she unloaded, "That selfish greedy little bastard!"

I walked toward her, "Please calm down. Who are you talking about?"

Her face was bright red, "That nitwit Roger Kirshmire quit today; no two weeks' notice, nothing, just this shitty little email." She held out a piece of paper to me.

I took the email and started to read it, "Where is he going?"

"Fox!" she gasped. "They are going to have our whole plan. He betrayed us."

I took a deep breath, "This is bigger than him, or Fox, or CNN or anybody else. Remember he has no idea what we have for Friday. What are they going to do, counter-program us with Donald Trump?"

She laughed, "Oh yeah, just so they don't get Donald Duck! Now that would really hurt us."

I reminded her of advice from one of my bosses at the local TV station I had worked at in Pittsburgh. With his thick Pittsburgher accent he would always say, "Nahhh, c'mon, dose guys dahn ere can't hurt us!" And true to form, no one can hurt you unless you let them into your mind and your heart. You can defeat any enemy with the truth. I guess that is what they call faith. Can you also defeat a disease with your mind? If Jesus could heal all those people, why couldn't he prevent his own death? Why do we return to sacrifice so much in our society?

Pagan man sacrificed something good to please the sun and rain gods. The high priests sacrificed goats in the temple. Could God have sacrificed his only son so that we can be without sin? Why couldn't God have forgiven us as he teaches us to forgive? We still have sin and good people die every day. We sacrifice our very best young men and women to fight our wars. We honor those whom we sacrificed in the name of our country's freedom; but, what about trying to figure out how to eliminate war? Why do our citizens have to die? Things don't seem to ever change. We keep doing the same things over and over without some great humane resolve. We needed to confront God on these issues.

44.   The Seventh Encounter

It was our seventh trip to room number 1313. Gloria sat with her arms crossed. We had been in the room for more than two minutes. The stillness got to both of us. Finally I said, "Maybe he's a no-show today?"

Then God spoke, **"Where were we?"**

Gloria asked, "You are God. Don't tell me you can't remember?"

"The end for the Jesus fellow, yes I remember. What do you want to know?"

"What was the motivation for his arrest?" I asked.

"There were two forces of evil working against this man. What happened in Jerusalem was the worst thing that could possibly happen to anyone. This was another example of the destructive influence of religion over government."

"You mean the temple high priests using their power politically?" asked Gloria.

God's voice got louder, **"Yes. Jesus wasn't arrested by the Romans, as John the Baptist was, he was taken by the Temple guards of the Sanhedrin."**

I asked, "And they were?"

"The Sanhedrin was an assembly of twenty or more men appointed in every city in the Land of Israel. This council had the power to pass judgment resulting in either conviction or exoneration. In this case the trial ended when they condemned Jesus to death."

Gloria asked, "Why would any church condemn someone to death?"

"Was there no one to defend Jesus of Nazareth?" I asked.

"Jesus was very quiet. He said little at his trial because he knew all too well that just as they turned him away in his youth, they would do it again. They kept asking him if he was the Son of God. He didn't respond

to their questions for fear that anything he said would make it worse. Then they turned it around and demanded that he deny he was the Son of God."

"That phrase — anything you say will be used against you — is part of our justice system today," I added.

Gloria piped in, "The Temple elders were rough on him. They must have been worried about something."

"Of course, he did not deny that he was the Son of God. The leaders of the temple then took this poor man to Pontius Pilate, the governor of Roman Judaea, and asked the governor for his endorsement of the death sentence. They told Pilate that Jesus had claimed to be the King of the Jews."

"Pilate could have said no," I offered. "He could have overruled the leaders of the church?"

"He didn't care about Jesus. He couldn't have cared less. Crucifixions were taking place by the

hundreds. There were even soldiers in the Roman army who were specialists at this grim, barbaric form of punishment. This man Jesus had gotten himself into a no-win situation. He was gaining quite a following and the leaders of the temple had to stop him. He was preaching that you didn't need to use the temple to connect with God. He was protester, or you might say, protestant."

Gloria asked, "You said that this was the worst thing, did you mean the crucifixion, or the miscarriage of justice?"

"Think about it. The temple leaders were given the task of determining whether this man would live or die. Who gave them that right? I never said, hey if anyone disagrees with you, cut his head off or burn him at the stake or nail him to a cross. I never said that. This was man playing God once again."

I wondered out loud, "They made it up?"

"Yes, and this is when it started. This is when they got a free pass and no one said 'Hey wait a minute. Who made you God?' And the disturbing thing, it didn't stop there."

Gloria pushed, "Hey, I don't want to ruin your crusade, oh, bad choice of words, but people of faith will want to know about the resurrection?" There was a pause. It's the pause right before someone is about to say something very significant.

"No. His body was stolen. Just like no one seems to know what happened to John F. Kennedy's brain. Let me give you the timeline: They put him on the cross, yes it was a Friday and that meant they had to remove him from the cross before sundown. In this case, sundown is when the Sabbath began. There was this rich guy name Joseph of Arimathea who slipped the guards some silver

and convinced them that he would put the dead guy in his personal tomb."

"This Joseph of Arimathea, he was a Christian?" I asked

God continued, **"Yes, but under the radar. Joseph of Arimathea took the body. And yes Jesus was dead when they took him down from the cross. Between the beatings to break his legs and the nails that were driven, not into his hands, but through his wrists, he was very dead. They employed five-inch nails through the victim's heels as well. Although you can take my word for it, this was recently proven by an archeological dig. Crucifixion was a rather repugnant remedy for silencing dissenters."**

Gloria uttered, "This is disgusting."

"The Romans wanted the locals to see how many people they nailed to the cross. They left them on the hill

as a deterrent to aberrant beliefs. These killings were just another result of men shifting between instincts, superstitions and misconceptions without regard for human life."

I asked, "But Jesus was on the cross for less than a day?"

"Yes, Roman corruption afforded Jesus a privilege. And of course, strange emotions bubble to the surface when loved ones die. Friends will do anything to make sure their loved ones are remembered in the most positive light."

Gloria added, "Yes, we never speak ill of the dead."

"In the dark of night, the followers of this wonderfully kind and poetic man came back to the tomb, opened it and took his body away."

I was aghast, "Why would they do that?"

"It was because they loved him. They didn't want anyone to come and take the body and parade it in the street, or burn it. Remember, they already believed he would live forever, so they already knew the outcome of his soul. They were protecting what they had left of their savior. Would you permit the body of your loved one to be in the hands of strangers to be dishonored, mocked and desecrated?"

"Nothing more than a martyr," Gloria added.

I jumped in, "Many idealists face the same fate but they don't generate a 2,000 year old religion."

"Yes but they don't have an army of devotees to go out into the world and spread the word. The killing of Jesus and the so-called resurrection helped to sell the message. They believed in their message as much as their Messiah. They knew they could talk to God whenever they wanted. But there was a problem with this plan."

Gloria asked, "What else could go so wrong in this macabre story?"

"It wasn't long before his followers ran into intelligent questions from people who wanted proof that Jesus was really the son of God. They needed to morph this virgin-birth, son of God story into something that would satisfy those who were on the fence. It was the sales job for the ages."

I asked, "The disciples and Paul couldn't control the belief in Christ as the son God?"

"There are always political forces that see that believing in a state and believing in a God could be merged together, harnessed and used to protect those in power. There were those men who felt the need to manipulate and mold a belief to favor themselves. Controlling what people believe has been the part-time

job of governments and fulltime job of zealots for centuries."

I asked, "Are you suggesting that once it started to snowball the disciples let the myth blossom?"

"It's like the time that Haile Selassie went to Jamaica for the first time. He was going to tell the Rastafarians that he was not the Savior they believed. But once he saw the crowds cheering, he decided to go with it. If they think you're a deity why disappoint them?"

Gloria took a very serious tone, "So, it's wrong to make people believe you are a god when you are not?"

"Those people knew they were lying."

45. The Romans Again

The room was getting some sun, so Gloria and I moved the chairs out of the glare. I offered this overview, "The birth wasn't a virgin birth, the man was a real man and he died at the hands of the Romans and Jewish leaders and he didn't go to heaven?"

"There cannot be a virgin birth. A woman becomes pregnant when a man's sperm penetrates her egg. Yes, Jesus was real and his body was taken away and hidden by his people. You used the word heaven. What do you really mean by that; where all the good boys and girls go?"

Gloria pepped up, "Do people have souls and do those souls go to heaven? Where is heaven?"

"There is no heaven. Does a person last forever? Well, in a chemical sense, yes. If you burn the body and scatter the ashes those atoms and molecules do go on forever. But I am afraid that this heaven thing is another

well-constructed myth. There is no heaven; not in the dark matter, not in the black holes, not anywhere. There is a force of the universe to be reckoned with, but the idea of some county club in the sky is a bit narcissistic."

I was flabbergasted, "So, what happens when you die? Is all this for nothing?"

God got forceful, **"Really? What is that? You were given life and a brain and feelings and you can spend your short time doing something good for yourself or good for someone you love. And if your belligerent righteousness doesn't get in the way, maybe you can do something good for mankind. Telling people there is a heaven has done zero to bring Jesus and Muhammad and other prophets' words into action. People are terrible to one another and the religious embarrassment started three hundred years after Jesus died."**

Gloria nudged me, "Romans, betcha it's the Romans again?"

"Yes the Romans. In the year 313, the Roman Emperor Constantine was the first leader to view Christianity in a positive light. Constantine was fighting his brother-in-law and was seeking divine assistance. He claimed he had a vision and ordered the shields of all his army have the Greek letters of Chi and Rho. It looks like an X and P on top of each other. Those are the first two letters of the word "Christ" in Greek."

I mentioned, "And his forces won the battle, thus his faith was solidified."

God added, **"As the popularity of Christianity increased the Romans decided to go with the flow. In 380 AD, Christianity became the state religion of the Roman Empire by the decree of the Emperor. And once again, the government was telling you what you will believe."**

I queried, "You sound like you have a problem with the Roman Catholic Church. Didn't they do a good job spreading Christianity to the world?"

"Oh, the Roman Catholic Church was all powerful, or as I like to call them: *the corporation*. Yes they spread Christianity all over the flat Earth and watched the sun go around the Earth, but that isn't all they did. The first thing they did was to translate the Bible into Latin. They got a bunch of so called religious leaders in a room and decided what to put in and what to leave out."

I added, "There is a Scottish saying that goes something like, *"show me the man who controls the lyrics of the songs of the country, and I care not who writes the laws of the land."*

Gloria slipped in, "Or the Psalms."

"The religion of the New Testament was translated and tailored to what "they" wanted the people to believe. If only Jesus had lived forever to guide the

Romans. They attempted to be democratic about the process. In 325 AD they had a meeting of the First Council of Nicaea."

I mentioned, "The Nicene Creed."

"Yes, and in this little creed, the Catholic Church put itself in a position of determining the details of believing. The church called upon its followers to say that they *believe in one God, the Father Almighty, Maker of heaven and Earth, and of all things visible and invisible.*"

Gloria kicked in, "Believing in the invisible; that would cover numbers, geometry and theoretical science."

"You are getting ahead of yourself, Gloria. But what the creed was asking is that all Christians had to believe that *Jesus is of one substance with God.* To codify that God and Jesus were the same. And they introduced this concept of a Holy Spirit of the Virgin Mary and expanded that into a belief in a Holy Ghost. I am God and I don't even know what that is."

I wondered, "Is it the word 'Ghost' that bothers you?"

God was very firm, **"Yes, and it should bother you. There are no ghosts. This was an attempt at explaining certain things away and giving the pagans that remained something to bite on. And they did. People of that day felt comfortable with the hypothesis that the Father, Son, and Holy Ghost were one thing. Before everyone's very eyes they created a trinity of gods. Nowhere in the Bible did it talk of a trinity; it was the work of the corporation. After all that Moses had done and all that Jesus had taught about one God, those guys walked backwards into the past. All progress was reversed."**

"The Catholic Church gave us all the pomp and symbolism," I commented.

"They have their statutes of a bleeding Jesus so everyone can look up and pray. They make the sign of the cross, the very symbol of man's lowest form of punishment. This was this man's worst day in his life and there they are parading the symbolism of torture to make people feel, what?"

Gloria asked, "You seem a bit angry with them?"

"That is only the beginning. When people went against them or presented a different viewpoint they were persecuted. The Church of Rome was scandalously relentless. Pope Martin V dug up John Wycliffe's body 44 years after he died to burn him at the stake."

Gloria was miffed, "Why? He was already dead?"

"It was because Wycliffe taught a more Bible-oriented viewpoint on Christianity. The Roman religious rabble kept the Bible from being translated into other languages for a thousand years because they wanted to keep their power over the common man who didn't speak Latin."

I added, "But there were people who finally translated the Bible into English."

"Like William Tyndale who translated the Bible into English and the Catholic Church gathered the books and destroyed them. They burned bibles because they were in English. And then in 1536 AD, they rounded up poor William and strangled him to death, and then, for good measure, burnt his body at the stake."

I had to add, "And Galileo spent nine-years of his life in house arrest because of his discovery that the sun was the center of the universe?"

Gloria added, "And in 1992, the Vatican finally cleared his conviction more than 350 years later."

"You've done your research. Fifty-thousand women killed in witch hunts from 1480 to 1750 AD. The

Inquisitions in Spain killed thousands, and in Europe, Muslims, Jews and even Christians that the Catholic Church didn't like were killed. More than 6,000 people were put to death in the name of the Lord during the Inquisition alone. They were the corporation of death."

Gloria added, "And the Templar Knights?"

"Yes, Pope Clement V was implicated in the arrests, torture and killing of the Templar Knights. They killed Joan of Arc and then made her a Saint. Who can really admire those power-hungry popes?"

"Well, they do seem to try to make things right," I suggested.

"Governments are no better. History shows that between 1914 and 1945 over 100 million people were killed in the two World Wars. The Vatican sat silently by as the Nazis loaded up six million Jews into trains that took them to their death. Where were their hunger strikes?"

I offered, "But there was a world court and people were charged and convicted of war crimes."

God spoke softly, **"And for hundreds of years they have been abusing children right in their churches and they have denied these crimes even in your court of laws."**

Gloria shouted, "WHY HAVEN'T YOU DONE ANYTHING ABOUT IT!"

There was an eerie silence for about a minute, and finally God spoke, **"If I was the God they conjured up in the Old Testament they all would be gone and burning in hell."**

46. Rounding the Bend

Even though I was in a timeless state, I felt like my time was running out. We only have so much on this Earth. I felt like we were almost ready for "A Week with God." Here I was sitting before my most important guest and we were a week away.

I wanted to focus the discussion, "We're coming down the home stretch here and I would like to move from the crucifixion of the Catholic Church and shift to another topic."

"Well, what next?"

Gloria asked, "What about the reform movement? Were people like Martin Luther and John Calvin real heroes in helping the church return to biblical values rather than Rome's dictates?"

God continued, **"Why do people always think reformers are good? Why would returning to the myths and arcane laws of the past be a good thing? Martin Luther did speak out. Martin Luther was excommunicated by the Pope for saying that the**

Indulgentiarum doctrina of the Catholic Church were wrong."

Gloria asked, "You mean the practice of selling forgiveness from sin?"

Yes, that is right. Luther nailed his Ninety-Five Theses to the door of an indulgence salesman in 1517. He also translated the Bible into German, so some say he was the father of the Protestant movement. He also said that the Muslim faith was a tool of the devil, but had no problem printing the Qur'an so that it could be read and analyzed."

"What about John Calvin, another reformer?" I asked.

God became rather animated, **"He was a horrible person. In his first five years of rule in Geneva, 58 people were executed for their religious beliefs. He exiled 76 others for the same reason. Not a good person."**

Gloria looked up, "You mention the Muslim faith. What do you think about Muhammad, the father of Islam?

"Yes, the man was a unique human being. He was another rebel with a cause. He was a good man who was as much a nationalist as a man of God. If you study the way he united all the tribes of Arabia you will understand the loyalty of the fundamentalists of today."

I spoke up, "Are you Allah?"

"It doesn't matter what you call me. There is only one God. Yes, same God. Christians, Jews and Muslims all believe in the God of Abraham. I am the God of all men."

Gloria asked, "Didn't Muhammad face persecution as well, just like Moses and Jesus?"

"Persecution is part of what you get when you are a visionary. Muhammad was born 570 years after Jesus. At the time of his birth, even some of the Arabian clans were

Christian. There were times when those who followed Islam were aligned with Christians. And believe it or not, Muslims also worked with Jews very productively. You see, Muhammad ibn ʿAbd Allāh did not read or write so his wonderful poem was conceived and then recited over and over. That is how he taught."

"He said you wrote it," Gloria probed.

"He was the wordsmith. I am only the inspiration. Consider the things he professed as law: First, that man should not kill female babies."

Gloria snapped, "Why women would let that happen is totally dumbfounding."

"In the early tribal tradition, they killed the newborn girls because they felt they didn't need females. They wanted men to fight and work. Remember a man could have more than one wife so one of the wives was always pregnant."

I interjected, "He was also concerned about the poor like Jesus."

"He made it clear that whether a man is wealthy or poor he is equal in the eyes of God. And he said that women should not be property. He put it this way, women are the twin half of men."

Gloria suggested, "He sounds like a reformer, in a way."

"He used to say seeking knowledge is the duty of every believer. When he entered Quba in 622 AD, he proclaimed: 'Spread peace – feed the hungry – honor kinships – pray while others are asleep, and you shall enter paradise,' and as we know, prayer is very important to all Muslims."

Gloria explained, "Praying five times a day is one of the five pillars of the faithful."

"Yes, the five: reciting the Muslim profession of faith, performing ritual prayers in the proper way five times each day, paying alms to benefit the poor, fasting during the month of Ramadan and making the pilgrimage to Mecca. Rather simple requests."

I wanted to know, "Where did it all go wrong? Was it the part about honoring kinships that was misinterpreted? Look at the Middle East. It's a disaster."

"If Muhammad would have lived forever there wouldn't have been such a problem. The Sunni and Shi'ite problem started with an argument about who would become the leader after Muhammad's death. And it continues. Muhammad would be repulsed by the killing in the name of the Qur'an."

Gloria pressed on, "How does a young man believe that if he kills in the name of his religion he gets 72 virgins when he gets to heaven. How could this motivate people to suicide?"

"Is not the men who start a religion. It's the men who come after who destroy the very fiber of what made that faith so valuable in the first place. Like the idea of making women cover their bodies and faces. It was based on how Muhammad demanded his 13 wives dress when they went out. He didn't want people to know which women were his wives. He feared that someone would seek retribution against him by attacking his wives. He had his enemies."

Gloria added, "And the concept of Jihad?"

"The spread of Islam in the early days was done so by force. His armies marched on towns and took the land and converted the residents. Muhammad united the Arabs into one nation, but he also introduced the duplicitous doctrine called Jihadi. The *greater jihad* was the inner struggle by a believer to fulfill his religious duties. There was also what he called the outer conflict. This was where jihad equated to the armed struggle against persecution and oppression. This was not a case of loving thy enemy. This was a mandate to kill anyone who stood in the way of your beliefs."

"So, it can go either way?" I suggested.

"Yes, of course. But you should remember there was a real Jesus connection with Islam. Muhammad mentioned Jesus in the Qur'an. He called Jesus the Messiah and God's gift to sinful man. He referred to him as the Savior, the Liberator, our Redeemer and the Savior of the world; a fairly strong backing. And he had great respect for scriptures and was unhappy when he saw people destroy them."

"Why do some Muslims have problems with Christians and Jews?" Gloria asked.

"Once again, things get crazy when land and power are involved. We go back to the Bible and the myth about the Jews being the descendants of Abraham's son Isaac. The Arabs are supposed be the descendants of Abraham's son Ishmael. The story says that Ishmael was the son of a slave woman while Isaac was the favorite son."

Gloria leapt, "The die was cast from the beginning. With words like 'chosen' and 'promised' and 'favorite' the Jews were setting themselves up for some genuine gentile jealousy."

"Yes, it is the weakness of man to crave being part of a group. Each group demands loyalty, a vetting process and membership fees. In principal, all groups that select their members are non-inclusive. Whether you are talking about the Jews, the Christians, the Muslims and the subdivisions of each group, the Sunni and Shi'ite, the

Protestants and the Catholics or the sects of Judaism something has to give. Once they put a capital letter on their name they are declaring their self-importance."

Gloria was making a strange face, "By the time Muhammad was born, the world population was 200 million people. Today, some estimates put the Muslim population of the world at 1.6 billion people. There are 1.3 billion Catholics in the world. Is this is going to be a pure numbers game?"

"Are you asking where this is all going? I would say this to mankind, be very careful who and what you believe in. There was a guy named Adolf Hitler who thought he was right, even bragged that he was invincible and infallible. There were many people in Germany who thought he was wrong, but no one spoke up. Never believe anyone who says they are infallible."

I added, "There are people being killed, kidnapped and coerced every day in the world."

"The question is, how can mankind stop it? Women being raped, people being tortured and human beings being controlled by those who believe they have the right to rule. Those self-appointed zealots are nothing but the product of one lucky sperm that penetrated their mother's egg. No different than any other human being. The men with the uniforms and guns control the world. Why should I intervene? There are no guarantees with mankind."

I wanted to tie it up for the day, "One of my favorite writers on the subject is a former nun named Karen Armstrong. In her book, The History of God she wrote: *Human Beings cannot endure emptiness and desolation. They will fill the vacuum by creating a new focus of meaning.* I ask you again, did we just make you up so we can feel better?"

"After next Friday's TV Show, you will know the answer."

47.   The Eighth Encounter

We had decided to go back downtown later in the day. It wasn't such a great idea, but we needed to know more. Traffic in the city, even with all the rules in place to cut down the number of vehicles in Manhattan, was pure gridlock. We finally got back to Alphabet City. As we entered the apartment, the smell of incense was in the air probably wafting up from one of the other apartments. It gave the moment a feeling of being in a Far East temple. I imagined Gloria in a colorful sari and I with a Nehru jacket.

And then God spoke, **"We are not in India, Mr. Bronck."**

The fact he was reading my mind meant he was real and that made me feel good. Just when doubt would enter my mind, he would do something to show me that he was there.

For Gloria it was different of course, "I don't know what you guys have been smoking, but last time I checked we're in New York. What's with the India comment?"

"Jonas was reacting to the smell of the burning incense."

"Yes it smells like someone is trying to cover their lunchtime toking," Gloria laughed knowingly.

I broke off the game and stated the reason for this special meeting, "God, I think we have to think about the show. We need to talk about how you'll present yourself."

Gloria chimed in, "What he is trying to say is you can't just be a voice coming from off camera. They'll laugh us out of the building. I mean that is something Jon Stewart does. He has this phony deep God voice talk to him when he does his camera three routine. Our audience is not going to buy it."

"Well, that makes sense. It all started when people looked to the sky. They could walk to the mountain, they could swim in the lake, but they couldn't touch the stars. They could only see them. Then man evolved and got smarter. And he created spaceships that could take people into the space. You are learning what is really out there. Man can land on other planets. You send ships to the edge of the observable universe to send back information,

but you still don't know what is beyond this universe. You only think you are getting closer and closer to learning the truth."

I started to think he was going off subject here and may have missed the question, so I suggested, "Yes. That's all true, but next Friday night you'll be talking to more than 100 million people and they'll want to see something they can hold onto and someone they can relate to."

Gloria added, "The bible says that you made man in your image. Is that true?"

"Am I black, or white or Asian? What do you think I look like? How can the force of the universe fill a human body? Do you want me to look like one of those gray extraterrestrials? Man is the product of 2.4 million years of evolution, while I am as old as the universe."

I caught that, "Then how were you created?"

"I wasn't created. I am infinity. Think about it. There are billions and billions of universes out there. The

same things that made the Earth and your solar system are making other universes every day, every second. You are not the first planet with people and you will not be the last."

Gloria interjected, "So we aren't alone?"

"All the planets with life go through billions of years and then their suns burn out and they perish. Your sun will go out one day as well. And then, I will be the darkness, the calm steady Dark Matter looking for my next protectorate."

"Well, great! What a positive spin God. Could you sugar-coat it for us?" Gloria quipped.

I advanced the concept, "Do you know the timetable? Do you know the future?"

"Yes, and so do your scientists. Most people don't listen to them. They think they are just making all this stuff up, like the cosmos and global warming. While the

myth believers read their Book of Revelation and believe that when the end comes they get to live forever because they belong to this special club. News flash, when the sun goes out, no one is saved."

Gloria asked, "Isn't your prognosis just as depressing and apocalyptic as what was written in the last book of the Bible?"

"Unless you can figure out a way to travel faster than the speed of light to get to some safe planet you will never survive. But this won't be the end of life. It'll only be the end of your brand of life."

"And here I am worried about what form you should take on TV," I said.

Gloria straight-faced, "No reason to stay on the diet, now is there?"

"What do people think God would look like?"

Gloria picked up her iPad and searched the Internet. She googled: What did Jesus look like and turned her iPad in the direction of God's voice, "Okay here you go. This is what they think Jesus looked like. This is the one that most Catholic grandmothers have hanging on their kitchen wall."

"He looks like a movie star. Why would they think Jesus looked like that?"

He piqued my interest with that comment, "And why would you say that?"

"All you need to do is look at a picture of Bin Laden."

Gloria jumped in, "What? With all due respect, was that your attempt at humor?"

"No, I am not being funny. Jesus looked very much like Osama, only he wasn't that tall. Think about it. Jesus was the son of a young woman from Nazareth and a Roman from Sardinia. Look into the eyes of Bin Laden and you can see why people followed him."

I couldn't believe what was I was hearing, "If you say that on TV people are not going to like you. Let's focus, what should you look like?"

"As long as you tell everyone that I have no form, no body, and no living cells. I am a magnetic field of energy and I would only take a form in order to help the small human mind focus on the meaning of my words."

Gloria suggested, "Why don't you come in the form of the Angel Gabriel? He seems to be the one who always pops up and talks to people. Isn't that who gave Muhammad the Qur'an?"

God blasted, **"There are no angels. Those are the creations of man. Those are part of the hallucinations of men who haven't eaten for days. Those are the images that gullible people see when they eat the wrong fruits or mushrooms in the wilderness. If you pray long enough and keep saying the same things over and over again you** can even believe that you are God. YOU ARE NOT GOD."

We left the room. The smell of incense was slowly leaving the air. As we got to the street Gloria turned to me and hugged me like a little girl hugs her father, "Jonas, I am afraid."

I held her tightly. I hailed a taxi. When we got into the cab I turned to her and said, "Don't be afraid. We'll figure this out. I don't think we can get out of this. We're at the point of no return."

Gloria said, "We may be at the fork in the road, or whatever cliché you want to throw at this, but I am just worrying about being able to pay the maintenance fee on my co-op after I lose my job. This lunatic is going get us killed."

48.   It Began

I forgot who said it to me early in my career, but it went something like this, "Open with a bang and finish strong." We had five really great shows planned for the week.

I was putting the final touches on the questions for the next show when Gloria came into my office, "Okay, I think I have an idea."

I pushed away from my desk and faced her, "Yes?"

Gloria with a large grin, "We have a candle on the table. When we start the show the candle is not lit and then when you introduce God, the candle lights. Just like when you first met him."

I was rather amazed. It was that simple. The image of a candle that the camera people can zoom in on and it can be the image we use in the bumpers for the show. Those are the little graphic slides that bookend the exit and return from commercials.

"This is genius," I added, "We have to be very clear and make sure some of guests who claim that God is all powerful use some kind of light metaphor. And we should point out that, just like the Islamic believers say, we are not worthy of even knowing what he looks like. And of course, the Jewish followers remember Moses and the burning bush."

Gloria added, "And Christians see Jesus Christ and God as the light."

"This is good," I was impressed.

Hours later I sat in front of three cameras while our theme song played and the special voice over announced: Now live from the TNN Studios in New York please join Jonas Bronck for "A WEEK WITH GOD!"

The Monday night show featured a panel of guests. One was a doctor of biology from a university in Ohio, Martin Karpinski. The second person was the main spokesperson for the Intelligent Design movement, Francis Bebe. And the third panelist was my friend Dr. Samantha Smith. I wanted to get the creation vs evolution debate on the table right out of the box.

I asked the first question, "Why is it so hard for Christian fundamentalist to buy into evolution? We have to remember the people who wrote the Bible thought the sun rotated around the Earth and the Earth was this small little flat parcel of land."

Martin took the torch, "They can't get it through their small little human minds that biology and the bible are not compatible."

I chimed in, "That's rather harsh. What's so wrong with the Bible?"

Martin continued, "For example, you can start with the book of Genesis. It talks about a dromedary camel being used by nomadic tribes 200 years before Jesus was born. Clearly the book of Genesis was written at a much later date and tacked on to the beginning of the Bible. Dromedaries don't get to that region until 100 or 200 years after Christ. That is the study of biology."

Francis Bebe made his move, "Let's not waste time on the exactitude of the Bible's observations and specifics. Really a camel? Let's focus on the fact that God made every living creature here on Earth and the first two humans. Adam and Eve lived in an idyllic place called the Garden of Eden."

I turned to Samantha hoping for something to inject, "Well, clearly, many of the passages of the Bible must be read two ways. Samantha isn't that true?"

Samantha smiled, "Jonas, the Bible can be taken literally. You can either see it as a story about man's viewpoint on what was happening at the time or interpreted as a poetic metaphor for how they thought things worked. Did the prophets such as Noah, Moses, Jesus and Muhammad really talk to God? Yes, we have to believe they did, just as God talks to anyone who is open to hear him."

I couldn't help but feel like she was talking right to me. Did she know something? Was she somehow connected to this whole thing and was warning me with her suggestion of things not being what they seem?

I turned back to Francis to light the fire, "Dr. Bebe, why the fight to have creation taught alongside of evolution in classrooms? Several courts have said that your belief is not a science, but part of religion. Some states have banned the practice."

Bebe leaned forward and raised his finger for emphasis, "What God created is irreducibly complex. No random mutation can create such wonderfully complex and functional things in the world. It was solely God's work."

I had to clarify, "You use the word *irreducibly*. So our audience understands that means impossible to transform into or restore to a desired or simpler condition.

In a sense, once each living thing was made by God it is the same as it was the day he made it, right?"

Francis Bebe continued, "Yes. Look at the complex petals of a flower or the human eye. They didn't evolve, they were created by God."

Karpinski leapt, "That's crazy. First of all take a look at all the breeds of dogs. Amazing that we can see the difference between a French poodle and Pit Bull, but we cannot see evolution. If we follow what you are saying Bebe that would mean that they haven't changed since God made them. But they have. That is why we call them breeds. They were bred by humans to take on different shapes, sizes, and colors. They were wolves some 50 million years ago and about 150,000 years ago we started to domesticate them. That's not very irreducible."

Samantha added, "Really Francis, the more we learn about evolution the more there is to teach our children how amazing God is."

I turned to Karpinski, "What about the human eye? Or the eye of any vertebrates?"

Martin Karpinski smiled like I set him up, "Not just vertebrates. Interestingly the evolution of the eyes of the vertebrate was different from the cephalopod."

"Martin you're referring to octopuses and squids, right?" I clarified.

Martin continued, "Yes, that's right. In the cephalopods, the light-sensitive cells are arranged so that the nerve endings of these cells are at the back of the eye away from the light; whereas in the vertebrates they are in front actually making the light pass though the nerves before the light gets to the cells. We humans actually have blind spots in our vision."

A frantic Francis Bebe demanded, "And what is your point?"

Martin looked up calmly, "That means, objectively speaking, the intelligent designer gave the guys with the muscular hydrostats, oh I'm sorry, the tentacles, the better designed eyes."

I interrupted, "Okay, we'll be right back to *A Week with God on TNN.*"

The floor manager announced, "Okay, we're out."

Francis Bebe looked at Martin Karpinski, "You're a real asshole Martin."

49.   The Ninth Encounter

The first show had gone better than I imagined. The Today Show did a story on what we were doing with "A Week with God." Fox mentioned us as well, with their usual slant. They accused me of being, get this, "pro-anti-God." Is that even a proper English phrase?

It was time for Gloria and me to make another trip to the apartment to make sure our little plan with the candle would be okay with God. When we sat down this time, Gloria noticed something was different. She pointed to the kitchen and toward the refrigerator. On the door there was a magnet that wasn't there before. Gloria walked over to the door and got a closer look. It was the magnetic card of a Chinese restaurant. Someone had put it there and she wanted to know, "Okay, who has been ordering Chinese food?"

"What is the matter with you two?"

I spoke up, "There is an indication someone else was in here. They put a magnet on the fridge door."

God replied, **"Someone was here yesterday. They were inspecting the place. They had clipboards and they**

took notes. They measured the rooms and they talked about ordering food. Then they got a call and left in a hurry."

It was very suspicious. All of a sudden I had fallen from my high 9 on the 'really God' scale back to my comfortable 7. I looked at Gloria. She shook her head slightly like you would when you were a hostage and wanted to communicate to another person without being noticed by your captors. Gloria spoke as she moved back to her chair, "So God, we were thinking about how to present you on Friday."

"Yes. It's a good idea. The candle is good. I will light it right before I speak for the first time."

I looked at Gloria with a sense of relief. I told no one else about her idea and I am sure she said nothing. We all have moments of doubt about our lovers, our family, our friends, our government and even our God. And then something happens to restore some faith. My notebook was almost filled to the last page with notes. I started the conversation on a controversial subject that was in the news a lot. I leaned forward, "One of the questions we're going to ask you is this whole thing about same sex marriage and the whole concept of homosexuality."

"People are challenged by anything a little different from what they expect."

Gloria perked up, "What do you mean?"

"I am saying people are confused. Desiring someone of the same sex is not new. Humans could have evolved so everyone was the same sex and that everyone could have the ability to make babies? Would that have made it better?"

"You mean like earthworms. They are hermaphrodites. Each individual worm carries both male and female sex organs," I offered.

"Yes, how did that happen? Why did that happen? With everything so neat and perfectly male and female in the world, how did these little slimy earth eaters get so confused? I certainly had nothing to do with it.

Homosexuality is a product of evolution and you see it in dogs and cats and cows. Sometimes people desire their own sex. Some people are born one sex, while knowing they should be another sex. Why do men have breasts? Rather useless unless they have a need to become a female later in their life."

"Never thought of that," I said.

"People on the Earth fight evolution? They fear what they don't understand."

"So, being Gay isn't a sin?" Gloria asked.

"Sin? I didn't write the laws and determine what sins are. Man does that. I only know what evil lurks out there in the deep universe. Why would anyone worry about such a thing as homosexuality? The next time some large asteroid slams into your planet it won't just hit the gay community."

I was drawn in once again, "What keeps that ultimate disaster from happening?"

"You might be a moving target, but look at the face of the moon. Those are not eyes in green cheese. Those are direct hits. People always ask why God is doing this to me when things go really badly. And then when they win the big game they thank God for making it all possible. As if I put all my energy into their team to keep the other guys from scoring. Now you see what I mean when I say silly humans, Gloria?"

Gloria pushed, "I get it, but who told the prophets what was bad or good? Was it just men writing out what they thought we should do?"

God got huffy, **"Again you are asking me if I spoke to them. You keep asking and I keep telling you the same answer. Why would I speak to them? They already had their minds made up about what they would write. They**

already had an idea of what was bad and good. You see you do not need a God to devise a moral code. Man wrote the Golden Rule way before the Bible. You can find variations on that same theme 4,000 years ago."

I closed my eyes, "Could the Bible be a work of plagiarism? Did the writers just misappropriate archaic myths and insert them into their story to unite their own group of people? I remember what you said before, but I just want to get our questions straight."

"Humans have always loved a great story, but when the hatred and violence of the storyline creates human suffering, man shows a weak side. When they use these stories or faulty lists of laws to commit murder, condone slavery and codify barbaric ways to control people that bothers me greatly."

Gloria blurted out, "What about abortions?"

"That will come up when we are on the air," I added.

"You justify killing so easily. You fly drones and drop bombs on someone you think is your enemy. When you find out that you killed a village of innocent people you say, I'm sorry, my bad. And then you send another drone to kill some more. And you rack up your errors as human collateral damage."

"That's war. I'm talking about a woman's right of deciding her own biology!" Gloria was very serious.

"Is that really what you are talking about? A woman and man go on a vacation and happen to get drunk and have sex and the woman gets pregnant. And the couple is planning on buying a new boat so they pay a doctor to end the life of the potential child. Is that just more collateral damage in their quest to have a boat and impress their friends?"

Gloria couldn't hold back, "What if the woman was raped? What if the woman had no means to care for the child?"

"That is ridiculous. You justify things with words. If you believed what the Bible said, both the rapist and the girl would be stoned to death; if the man would ever be found guilty. Is that any more logical than killing a potential child? You kill because you think it will solve problems. You have your answer before you and you refuse to see the truth. Killing human beings is wrong?"

I attempted to de-emotionalize the conversation, "But our society has come to the conclusion that life doesn't really begin at the point of conception, or fertilization."

God reflected my calm demeanor, **"You can't have things both ways. You cannot say you believe in evolution and then, refuse to let nature take its course. You have no idea if that fetus will be your next Messiah or your next** serial killer. You use evolution as your science and then use a myopic viewpoint to legislate when life begins. What you cannot comprehend you blame on God or wave your Constitution in the other person's face. You want to play God? Go ahead, play God and kill the baby."

"Are you saying that abortion is a sin and it is wrong? I am confused." The look of disappointment spread across Gloria's face.

"If you believe what you say you really believe in you wouldn't need to ask God what is right. You would just fix it yourself. If you truly believe that killing is wrong, why do you keep killing? It seems strange that you don't see that there are so many couples who cannot have children. And those people have to go to other lands to adopt babies. You don't seem to comprehend that killing your species never solved any problem. You equate ownership of property and biological control. You will decide that ending a life is more important than the freedom of that one specific life. Abortions, wars, executions, mercy killings, it's all the same. It's simply your reptilian brain winning."

50.   The Tenth Encounter

The second night kind of misfired. The idea looked so good on paper. We wanted to have a strong expert on Christianity, a Jewish scholar, a Buddhist monk of great reputation and a highly respected imam based in New York City. What we ended up with were four people who kept selling why their dogma was the true faith. The Daily News ran a picture of the men walking into our studio with the headline: Where's the Bartender? A reference to those jokes that start out, "a rabbi, a priest and a monk walk into a bar." In the TV business the maxim that any publicity is good publicity had to be applied here.

On the way to the apartment on Wednesday morning my phone news alert system started to beep. There was another early morning school shooting. Deeply disturbed by the number and frequency of the shootings in schools and universities, I wondered what Moses, Jesus or Muhammad would say of such carnage. Of course, today we had another chance to talk to God.

Gloria opened this morning's session, "A lot of people my age have tattoos, but I noticed in Leviticus 19:20 it clearly states *"do not cut your bodies for the dead or put tattoo marks on yourself."*

I offered, "I think she is asking what you think about tattoos?"

"We've been over this before. Those are not my words, but if you must go there, we can talk about the mixed messages in that historical document."

"We're talking the Bible here?" Gloria asked.

"Yes, where they keep saying – God said this, or God said that – it's really them saying it. I thought you'd be asking me about the school shooting. But let's keep going, you were quoting the Bible."

"Okay," I pushed, "Why did they say that?"

"The world's population came out of Africa. As the migration started up into the fertile valleys of the Middle East, the Jewish flock didn't want to be associated with the African culture."

Gloria pressed, "What does Africa have to do with what the Bible says?"

"As early as 8,000 years before the birth of Jesus, Sudanese and Ethiopian tribes placed plates into their lips to establish social order in their group. Another thing was ear stretching to ward off evil spirits and some males thought it was some kind of sexual enhancer."

Jonas relates, "Yes, I have seen pictures. It looks painful."

"Painful, yes, and so was forcing young boys and girls in Sudan to undergo massive scarification by the tip of a red-hot knife. They were branding their children like cattle. The Jews wanted nothing of that."

Gloria suggested, "The Jews were an advanced civilization?"

God erupted, "Oh yeah, but those dichotomous Jewish leaders blamed me for a lot of bad things. How advanced were they when in Genesis they portray a conversation I had with Abraham. This is when I allegedly told him that every male among you shall be circumcised as a pledge between us. They call it a covenant with God. They had rules in the Bible that said you should not cut yourself. There is cutting involved in circumcision."

"I guess Jesus was circumcised, too. Didn't the Jews invented circumcision?" Gloria asked.

"No not at all. As they say, circumcision is the world's oldest elective surgery procedure. It started 25,000 years ago. Men did it to themselves originally, and then, they did it to their captured enemies, a kind of a present. Hey, we captured you, now take this."

"Wasn't it for health reasons? You know cleanliness?" I asked.

"Well I guess you could say that, but men very early on realized that a man who was circumcised seemed to get more oral sex. Women felt they were cleaner and smelled better."

Gloria gasped, "That's gross."

"You asked and besides don't you see a trend here of people and pain. When the Greeks and then Romans took over in the Middle East, they weren't too happy about this ritual of removing the foreskin. Leaders like the Greek King Antioctius Epiphanes in 175 BC outlawed the practice of circumcision."

"I'm sure that didn't sit too well with the Jewish population?" I asked.

"No it did not. They stayed angry about it for more than 300 years. It was one of the reasons they fought the Jewish-Roman wars in 132 AD in Judea."

Gloria pepped up, "Yes, the Bar Kokhba Revolt."

"Yes it was and it was partly caused by Romans not wanting to be circumcised. Almost 600,000 Jews were killed, 58 towns were taken over and 985 villages razed, destroyed, totally eliminated."

"A senseless war," I said.

God raised his voice, **"All wars are senseless, Mr. Bronck. If I did create man in my image, as the Bible says, then this would mean that I do not like the way my penis turned out. Not something an intelligent designer would admit. Human bodies don't need to be altered."**

Gloria asked, "So, tattoos are out?"

"People will do what they want. Having ink injected under their skin, inhaling smoke and tar, eating bad food; so much for that statement: My body is my temple. What is important here is no human being should ever be forced to have their bodies altered without

their permission. There are some positive alterations science has given mankind, like repairing harelips, correcting spines and clubfeet. That's different than circumcising eight day old male babies. Or worse, when men circumcise women in order to dull their sexual pleasure. "

"God is against circumcision?" Gloria asked.

God rebuffed, **"I didn't say that, I just think that people should decide when they are old enough to decide for themselves. Think why tribes disfigure their members. They do it for such inhumane reasons. Like Chinese women wrapping their feet to keep them small so they walk in short steps to please their men."**

"Yes, that is horrible." Gloria said.

"Or like women putting round wooden blocks in their ears, lips and noses to make them less attractive to

other tribes. Why would they do that? Were they really afraid that men from other tribes would steal their women?"

"Like the burka?" Gloria asked.

"Yes that is another example of man's insecurity and his desire to control women. It happens in every culture. I never told anyone to cover their heads. I really don't care if women want to show their faces, figures and heads in public. And really, may I offer, please get rid of that inane yarmulke. I know why this was invented. It was just a way to cover male-pattern baldness. What is this with the hats? Vanity is such a weakness in humans."

Gloria added, "I'll buy the best looking candle for the show."

51.   The Eleventh Encounter

Gloria and I had lunch in my office. We just finished contacting all the guests for that night's show. We used to call it "bed check." We needed to make sure everyone was in town, at their hotels and aware of what time we expected them to be at the studio. We were going over some of the notes when Gloria looked up and without warning said, "We have to go back there now."

I was alarmed by this sudden, almost mystical pronouncement. I put down my sandwich and looked at her, "Why now?"

Gloria said, "Just go with it. Call it women's intuition if you like. Let's go. I sense something is wrong."

We were out the door, down the escalators and into a cab within minutes. We got to the apartment rather sweated up due to broken air conditioner in the taxi. We buzzed through the lobby and up to 1313.

Gloria spoke first, "Why are you upset? You sent me some kind of message. Are you distraught? We need to work this out before you go on the show."

"Yes, I was thinking about you and I wanted you to know that I am very bothered by the phrase — *Act of God*. We have to discuss this on the show."

"Okay, why is that?" I calmly asked.

God continued almost in a whiny kid kind of way, **"I feel unjustly accused. This is how Jesus felt when he was brought before Pilate."**

"Please God," Gloria demand, "We didn't come all the way downtown to get cryptic here. What exactly are you talking about?" She wiped some sweat off her freckled forehead.

"Insurance companies use that phrase so that they don't have to pay a claim. A storm hits a town and it's so violent that a tree falls on a car and they say that isn't covered by their policy."

"Really?" I was miffed by this human-like behavior. I felt his credibility crumbling, "It's called Force Majeure. It's a common clause in contracts that frees both parties from liability due to some extraordinary event. It's something that is described by the legal term *act of God* like a hurricane, flood, earthquake, or say, a volcanic eruption."

God, now more animated, **"Well that bothers me. Why do they blame me? Hurricanes, floods, earthquakes and volcanos have been explained by your scientists. Why do you keep claiming God does them? Someone should sue the insurance companies and make them prove there is a God, which there is, and then prove that God is some great destroyer. I am angry that man uses my name in vain like that."**

I had to say, "Are you saying that the legal system is breaking one of the commandments? I must admit, I never thought of it that way."

Gloria moved us forward, "People need to know what your acts are. Who created the universe? Is anyone in charge? Or are we just on our own here, guy?"

"I told you it happens every day. Somewhere in the vast infinite space there is another big bang happening; another universe being created from nothing. Why do you always have to have a reason for everything?"

Gloria added, "Then, let's talk about origins. How did we get from single cell life forms to complex animals and then the human form?"

"Yes, I'm still unclear what your role was in the development of living things?" I asked.

"When you have 14 billion years lots of stuff can happen. Here is a little experiment. Right before you go on a two-week vacation spit in your toilet and then put a sun lamp focused on the toilet bowl."

"And this is for?" Gloria queried.

"When you get back from vacation you will be surprised to learn that things are growing in your toilet. That is how easy it is to grow single-cell bacteria. Now imagine that your vacation is a one-year long. You would be amazed how much organic material will be growing in the toilet. You see if you have enough time you can grow amazing things; like cheese left too long in your refrigerator."

"Water is important, but not light. Mushrooms grow without light." I suggested.

"Water is always important. It is amazing to me how you can pump oil in a pipeline for thousands of miles, but you don't have any way to pump water from the wet parts of the world to the farm areas affected by drought. You haven't figured it out. Water is very important."

I leaned forward and asked, "Why did man get the bigger brain and the greater intelligence than other animals? Was that, as much as you hate the term, an act of God?"

"If dinosaurs were nature's bad prototype, then man was evolution's biggest mistake."

Gloria spoke with loud passion, "A mistake? Why are *we* the mistake?"

"Because you had the potential of being the ultimate living creature, but you got caught in the dilemma of polarity."

"Polarity? What does that mean?" I asked.

"The Earth has a north pole and a south pole. There is the scientific notion of magnetism; the force that draws certain things to it, but pushes other things away."

Gloria pushed forward, "How can polarity of a magnet have anything to do with man's development on the Earth?"

God became frustrated, "The fact that humans are stuck between their primal subconscious urges and their objective reality based on knowledge and experience."

I pressed him, "Would you please give some examples?"

"Man believes he is an advanced creature, but is continually worried about threats to his land. What does he do? He kills. Faced with a lack of food on a mountain, he will eat another human being to survive. Man will always return to his primal instincts. Think about how many great leaders have been brought to their knees by their primal sexual attractions."

Gloria suggested, "Lots of people are brought to their knees, but on the good side, they have this instinct to protect their family. They not only have the goal of reproducing, but also of keeping their species alive. They provide food. What's wrong with all those things?"

"You are citing the good things, but there are some other dark things in there. When a volcano or hurricane destroys and kills some people, those who survive blame themselves. They carry survivor's guilt."

I proposed, "Surely that is learned, not pre-wired?"

"Oh, you are naïve. One's pre-wired need to survive is so important that people start to believe that they have the power to overcome anything. When they feel helpless in the face of a lava flow they quickly turn for help from a force above them. It's the old blame assignment. They ask, if I didn't cause this then who did?"

Gloria jumped in, "They create some super power and assign the disaster to that form."

"Yes, and they built their myths around these deities. Early man was more creative. They had many gods so they were very busy pleasing many. As time moved on man's improving logic delivered a desire to become more efficient so he narrowed it down to one God. If you asked anyone today whatever happened to the Sun God they would laugh at you."

I stated, "And they fought for the right to worship one God."

"This was very important to mankind. Man wanted a sense of order and control so they demanded that everyone get in line. They created myths and if you didn't go along with the crowd, you were told you would be sentenced to an eternity of burning pain in a place called Hell."

Gloria suggested, "The need in any story to have a hero and villain. They teach us that in order to have drama you must have conflict."

"Once you get it whittled down to one God you have to create this Devil character for people to visualize the conflict more clearly. Personification is man's ultimate ego. You must fashion everything in your image to make a belief work properly."

"Man seeks leadership. Man wants to follow someone," I said.

"Sure, so you elevate your prophets like Moses, Jesus or Muhammad to special status. Even modern day revisionists like Joseph Smith and L. Ron Hubbard should be put under a microscope. It's the same heroes and villains conflict that writers have been exploiting for thousands of years to bilk millions out of the less aware. The polarity of goodness and evil has to be part of the human belief system. It's pre-wired."

"Do dogs have souls?" I asked.

"Every living thing has feelings. We are all connected on a chemical, atomic level. All humans are made of the same stuff; it's just rearranged in what you've mapped as DNA. It will take another one hundred-thousand years for mankind to breed out his need for a Supreme Being."

Gloria peered into the space, "So, animals should not be killed. What would we eat?"

"You are a foolish people. You put a man in jail for two years for killing dogs, while his neighbor comes home with a dead deer strapped across his truck. You call it 'putting down' your pet when you kill them. You use language to justify what you do. What you haven't been able to reckon with is not the acts of God, but the acts of man. The acts of man will destroy mankind, not some psychotic's prediction in the book of Revelations."

"Please tell me we are not doomed," I pleaded.

"On a day when innocent children and teachers were gunned down, you ask me that? If man spent as much time on feeding people, teaching people, and using wealth to really make a better human experience for more people, there just might be a chance. Fanatically chattering about God is a useless endeavor. You have all the answers. Stop praying to me for things like your kids getting into that private school and get out there and do something positive to make the world a better place. Stop killing. Put away your guns."

"You're against guns?" Gloria asked.

"If I was the all-powerful God they say I am, I would eliminate every gun in the world. The only thing that will stop a bad man with a gun is for all guns to go away. Man will never give up his weapons. They are his metal testicles."

"Well that pretty much sums it up." Gloria put her pen down.

52.   Almost There

The third night was explosive. With two congressional representatives, one Republican and a Democrat and a woman from the Food Bank of New York, the conversation was potent. The premise was simple, if God was in Congress would he be a Democrat or Republican? Dennis Ianni was the Republican from California and Margret Wilkerson from Maine, the Democrat. The Food Bank president was Bethany Frostburg. I didn't even have to light the fire.

Frostburg started, "If God came to the United States, he wouldn't even be seen with anyone from Congress. He would clear you out like money changers in the temple."

Representative Ianni followed, "You really shouldn't throw stones when you live in a glass house Mrs. Frostburger."

Margret came to the rescue, "Now Dennis, play nice."

I jumped in as well, "Mr. Ianni, I believe her name is Frostburg."

Ianni kept at it, "We have looked into your accounting principles over there at the food bank and the

IRS would certainly like to know where $1.3 million went last year."

I had to stop this, "Representative Ianni, we aren't here to talk about the accounting and bookkeeping of the Food Bank. Margret Wilkerson, how many years have you been in Congress?"

"I am proud to say I've been in Congress serving my state for more than 20 years." Wilkerson smiled.

I kept the focus, "And in 20 years, how many bills have you proposed to help the homeless or help feed the poor?"

"Well, I must say I lost count, but probably more than 30," The congresswoman answered.

Bethany Frostburg interjected, "And none of them have passed."

"Is that true?" I asked.

Margret sadly answered, "Yes, no one cares about the poor."

I turned to Dennis Ianni and all I had to do was nod and he started, "Look that is unfair and ridiculous. We care about poor people, but we want them to find their own way.

If they just pull themselves up by their boot straps and get out there and get a job they can have a better life."

Miss Frostburg pounced, "Until they do get that better life do we just let them starve in the streets? Is that the Republican way of treating people fairly?'

"Dennis, Margret, Bethany, if God was voting on these bills how would he vote?" I asked.

Margret Wilkerson suggested, "Well, it isn't as simple as that. I don't believe God would want us to spend money we didn't have."

Frostburg shook her head, "Really, according to a study done by a Harvard professor the war in Afghanistan drained almost $4 trillion from the taxes we all paid. Along with the medical costs from all the returning wounded the whole affair over there in the Middle East cost the American public more than $6 trillion. So, yes, you are right Congresswoman Wilkerson, daddy spent all the money on his war looking for weapons of mass destruction."

The veins in Congressman Ianni's neck bulged, "You're one misguided young lady. If you think I'm going to sit here and not defend my country you're crazy. As a matter of fact, suggesting anything other than spending the money to protect the homeland is treasonous."

Wilkerson tried to calm it down, "Dennis, why are you attacking this lady? She has a point, we wasted a lot of money and too many lives, but I must admit I did vote for the war. We all did. It just seemed right at the time. We believed what we were told."

I asked, "So, is there a right time to feed the poor? Jesus said it. Muhammad said it. What are we waiting for?"

"Please do not quote Muhammad to me. He is not my God." Ianni sternly stated.

I looked him in the eye, "Muhammad wasn't a God, he was a prophet. You might want to know what he said before you judge him by the actions of those who have distorted his teachings."

Ianni continued, "I have all the proof I need in those two buildings here in New York and the Pentagon and that sacred field in Pennsylvania. I have seen what has been done with his teachings."

Margret Wilkerson filled with alarm, "Dennis STOP! We cannot rebuild human trust when we keep using fear and misinformation to promote a war state. I cannot believe you."

I looked at Bethany who was shaking her head, "Anything to add Miss Frostburg?"

She looked at me then right into the camera, "I know I am in the right country and I know I am on the right show, but I do not know why people who live like kings can't see that they are the solution to poverty and hunger. They need to figure out how to share the wealth."

I took it from there, "Okay, we'll be right back to A Week with God on TNN."

The video from the show was lifted and put on YouTube by hundreds of people. The video went viral and within hours we were looking at more than 25 million views. We were getting close to exploding.

53.   The Twelfth Encounter

The show Thursday night with Richard Dawkins, Michael Shermer and Sam Harris was over-the-top great. Because the special was pushed back due to the Malaysian airliner story, Dawkins was able to join us. With three of the top atheists I didn't have to do much talking. The show blew out the phones. Since we couldn't take calls, we just sat there for hours examining every aspect of God and their persuasive case against God existence.

Friday morning I called Gloria to make sure she was ready for one more trip to the apartment, "Good morning, how are you holding up? It's been a crazy week."

She sounded a bit nervous, "I'm fine; just running a little late. Can I meet you there?" She assured me that everything was okay, so I went about packing up all my notes for the final encounter with God before the big show. I wondered if there would be any contact with God after the show.

Today I wanted to find out what his top goal was for coming on the show. If he was truly non-human, then he couldn't possibly care what people thought about him. A last test was to find out if he showed any indication of wanting to kowtow to an audience.

I got to the apartment and sat down. He spoke first, "Where is Gloria?"

I cleared my throat and said, "She is running late. She'll be here shortly."

God spoke, "Fine, I guess; we're all set for tonight?"

I nodded, "Yes, we're ready. You understand the time? 8 p.m. and in case I didn't mention it the boss has cleared out all the commercials. So it's just you and me for three hours."

God said, "Yes of course. I understand. What else?"

He seemed uneasy. Was it the fact that Gloria wasn't there yet or was something else going on? I moved it along, "Well, I wanted to know what your major goal was? What do you want to accomplish? Is there one big point you want to make toward the end of the show?"

God continued, "Not really; I am sure you have all the right questions. You are very good at what you do. I'm sure it will be fine."

He seemed almost detached from it all. Just then there was a knock at the door. I got up and answered it. It was Gloria. She came in and apologized for being late.

God spoke, **"That is fine. I am glad you are here."**

As soon as she sat down I could hear a change in his voice. It was almost as if he needed both of us to be normal.

I began our last session with my first question, "There will be so many people who will be watching who will want to understand what a miracle is. If I ask you on live TV about things that people consider to be miracles, what are you going to say?"

"There are no miracles."

Gloria added, "What do you tell the woman who thought she had breast cancer and prayed for months and then doctors told her the cancer was gone?"

"I would tell her that she is a very lucky woman. How about this one, a plane took off from one of your airports in New York. Both engines sucked in some geese. The plane flew, but only barely. The pilot, an experienced aviator, landed the plane in the Hudson River. The temperature was about 20 degrees and all these good

Samaritans came to the rescue of the people on the plane. As soon as they saw the airliner land on the water, they came in their boats. They got to the plane and from the naked eye it looked like the passengers were standing on water, like Jesus walked on the water. They were actually standing on the wing of the plane. Everyone survived. And you called that the miracle on the Hudson. That wasn't a miracle. That was one good pilot and lots of lucky people."

I extended the point, "You used the biblical term *Good Samaritan*; interesting."

"You can think what you want. You've already told me about the woman who cured her cancer by praying. That wasn't in the bible. And I told you about the airplane, not in the Bible. And then there is the guy who prayed so hard he won the lottery. Believe me in 300 years they will be writing about a basketball player named Michael Jordan who could miraculously fly."

"Do you decide when people die?" Gloria asked.

God firmly answered, **"No. The way nature works is, you let it work. You are living on a ball floating through space. The inner core of your planet hasn't even cooled in 14 billion years and you ask me if I decide when people die? Things die. That is part of nature. Even species become extinct. People die."**

I liked where this was going so I asked, "Why did the dinosaurs come before man?"

"They were mutation of lizards and salamanders. The ones that survived became birds. If anyone wants proof about evolution look at the dinosaurs. Gravity on the Earth was slightly less back then so they grew so big. When the asteroid hit it bumped the Earth into a slightly

different rotation and the result was the gravity you have today. But the dinosaurs were gone."

"When did the asteroid hit?" I wondered.

"That was 65 million years ago. It's like gambling. The odds say that about every 100 million years the Earth will take a hit from a major piece of rock. There is a chance for another big asteroid to hit the Earth. You know, they travel at the speed of 17,000 miles per hour."

Gloria asked, "There are over one hundred million species on the Earth and in the life of the planet we've had more than a thousand times that number go extinct. Are we on that list?"

"Yes! Sorry. And yes, there could be an Earth one day with nothing but cockroaches and rats patrolling Wall Street. The only suggestion is to make a list. What are the things you can do to make sure that doesn't happen? You know so much about science and chemicals

and the way the Earth works. Why do you keep doing the same things over and over to destroy what you need to live on?"

"We're trying to get pollution under control, but some governments are worried about how that will affect their economy," I said.

"If you could have seen the Earth a million years ago, smelled the air, drunk the water, and seen the vegetation? No gas stations, no pollution. It was almost like a garden of Eden."

"We do have to save our planet," I said.

"Does man have a choice between salvation and damnation?" Gloria asked.

"I cannot save you. An intelligent human being knows it is all just chance and fate. And the reason you can talk to me today is because of fate and chance. You could be on Mercury, or Mars or Venus. Funny how you

gave your planets ancient god names as if you sent them out there, far away from your planet, to be forgotten."

"We've progressed from those pagan beliefs," I suggested.

"You used to pray to the sun god. What did that get you? All the old gods died and all those who believed in them have perished, but life goes on. Gloria, there is no salvation and the good news, there is no damnation. No one goes anywhere, but back into the uncountable number of atoms that make up everything. Enjoy the ride. It's certainly the only one you get. I am a realist. I am real."

Gloria smiled, "Good news. No hell."

54.   Show Time

When I do lectures to journalism classes I always pound preparation as the key to any successful story or interview. I watched people like David Frost, Mike Wallace, and Barbara Walters get the most out of people. I knew that endless preparation was at the root of their successes. I felt that we had done our work. Gloria wrote down every comment and put together a list of possible questions. She had an interesting model she used. She averaged the number of words a person used to answer a question and then figured out how many questions and answers could fill an hour. We had no commercials for this three-hour special, but we did have promos we could cut to if necessary. We took the long list of over 200 questions and narrowed them down to the 75 best.

We set up lighting and camera shots around 6 p.m. We had the lighting people in early because we wanted to try out the candle bit. We needed to be able to pick up the burning candle with two different angles: Straight on and one to the side. One of the camera guys had this great idea. He suggested we suspend one of those GoPro cameras from the light grid looking down on the whole set. The light coming from the candle produced a glowing effect in the fish-eye lens. It was really cinematic.

Gloria worked on the intro of the show with the teleprompter person and we were almost there by 7 p.m. I asked them to rack the script so I could do a read through from my position at the desk. The candle was replaced with a brand new one and was placed on the desk across from me. The set had lots of greens and blues. The candle was red so it really stood out. I read through the open and then, took a break in my office. As I sat there with my question cards in my hand, I thought how ironic that tonight would be my 13th encounter with God. I thought about how lucky I was to be doing this interview.

Gloria burst into my office holding her phone, her eyes welling up, "Oh my God Jonas, Steve is dead!"

I looked at her. She was reading the rest of whatever was on her phone. I kept going through my mental rolodex of people I know and tried to pull up a person with the name Steve. Then it hit me, "What? What are you saying?"

Gloria opened her mouth and with voice cracking, "Steven Summerville was found dead in the woods somewhere in Minnesota. Dead of an apparent shotgun wound."

I tried to stand up, but my legs wobbled. I sat back down, my mind raced through this information. I tried to piece it together. I thought about why he was in Minnesota and the conversation about his son. I visualized a shotgun in his hands. I looked at Gloria, "That's terrible, absolutely terrible."

"What are we going to do?" Gloria asked.

Now with some strength back in my legs I stood up, "We have to do the show. We must do this show. Let's rewrite the open."

The next 40 minutes seemed like a dream sequence in a movie where everything is shot through some cloudy effect and some parts are in slow motion and some of the sound is distorted. I don't even remember walking to the studio, sitting down, or getting prepped. I saw the clock in the studio read: 7:59:42.

The floor director barked out, "Places, everyone." A few seconds went by, and next I heard, "Ten seconds to air!" I saw his fingers below the lens of camera counting down; five, four, three, two and then he pointed and the prompter rolled,

"Good evening ladies and gentlemen. I'm Jonas Bronck and we offer you this final chapter in our series 'A

Week with God on TNN.' It is with heavy hearts we come to you tonight. We have just learned the President and CEO of the Triangle News Network, Steve Summerville, has passed away. Early reports say that Steve was the victim of a hunting accident in Minnesota. Steve was vacationing there. We will give you more on this tragedy when details become available. From our TNN family to Steve's family and loved ones we send our deepest sympathies and our prayers go out to you."

There I was on national TV, connected to a worldwide feed that was going out to more than 100 million people. All the preparation seemed senseless now. I had the teleprompter, like a teddy bear to comfort me in my time of need, the scroll started to roll again and I returned to the script.

"Tonight we have a special program. I know that we have discussed a lot this week about whether God exists. Whether there was an intelligent designer who put all that we see together. Did we have a creator? Is there an omnipresent, omnipotent, all knowing Father who helps us thorough each day, keeps us safe and teaches us the difference between right and wrong? Do we live in a world of chance and happenstance, or do we play out every move orchestrated by some great puppeteer in the sky?" I paused and took a deep breath, "For the last three weeks in preparation for this show I have been meeting with a force — an un-seeable force — who has taught me much about who we are and what our ancient scrolls really mean. Across from me you see a candle. It's not just any candle. That is a symbol of God." I looked down at the candle and gave the director some time to focus on it for effect.

Then I continued, "The God of Abraham that Jews, Christians and Muslims of the world follow and worship as the one and only God will be in our presence tonight. This is not a trick or hoax or prank. This, ladies and gentlemen is our chance to talk directly to God. If you have ever asked the question what you would ask God, if God could talk, this is your night. Call your friends, Tweet your followers, text your buddies, and tell the world that God is on TNN. With the due respect, let's all bow our heads and say a prayer. We will keep our cameras on the candle. God will light it when he is ready."

The camera focused on the candle then a close-up of the wick then the shot from above. The time seemed forever. I kept one eye on the candle. We were now more than 30 seconds into this which in TV time seemed like an eternity. Nothing. I kept thinking, "Come on God, this is no time for extra drama." We were now at one minute. This was unbearable.

I could hear Gloria's quickening breath in my ear piece and then her whispering voice, "What is happening Jonas?"

I waited for twenty more seconds and then I broke the silence, "God is here with us. Those who believe know that he is here. Call us now, at 1-800-GOD-ONE and let's talk about God on TNN. We'll be right back."

Gloria was in my head, "What happened?

I talked into my microphone, "Just line up the calls. We have to fill three hours. Get some promos racked up and make sure they have the 13 second delay on."

Always the pro, Gloria took control of the machine. During the promo I reached over the desk and lit the candle with a lighter. One of the camera guys gave me the thumbs up.

When we came back on air they took a close up of the candle now burning bright. I took the first caller who went on and on about how great it was to be able to profess his love for the son of God, Jesus and the Holy Ghost and proceeded to tell the world that being a Christian was the only way. After three hours of dogmatic calls, I was worn down. I just sat there nodding my head and going with the flow of the calls. I couldn't wait to get out of that chair and down a good stiff drink. I felt betrayed.

55.   The Aftermath

When I got to my office Gloria was standing by my desk with two glasses of scotch. She handed me a glass, "Here drink this and then you and I are going downtown." I sat down in the chair, in a daze. It was like someone let all the air out of a balloon.

Gloria could see the stress and despair in my face, "I could say something really stupid right now, like, *My God, My God, why have you forsaken me?* But, I am not immune to lightning strikes."

I stood up and took half the whisky into my mouth and swallowed. Blew out some air and moaned, "What a fucked up day."

Gloria downed the scotch like a Norfolk sailor on leave. She tried to cheer me up, "You know I did like the fact you lit the candle. That was a nice touch." I took the rest of the scotch, and then asked, "Is there anything good that can come from this?"

"Well the good news you only wasted 156 seconds of your life talking to that chicken-shit," Gloria smiled.

I threw my notes in my bag, "Let's go. I think someone really has some explaining to do."

We got out of the studio and down to the street and hailed a taxi. We gave the driver the address and sailed down Broadway. Around Times Square the lights were so bright it felt like day. We got to the apartment building and went into the lobby.

This time the doorman was not a familiar face. He stopped us as we approached the desk, "Good evening, may I help you?"

I fumbled for the key and while explaining who I was. I held the key up to his face.

He made an entry in a notebook on the desk, "Well, I think I know who you are. You're that TV guy, right?"

I answered, "Yes, Jonas Bronck. We have a meeting in apartment 1313. He's expecting us."

The doorman put the pen down and looked up with a stoic face, "That's one of those antique keys before the place was remodeled. That's from when this place was a hotel."

I got a little frantic, "Yes, we know that. We just need to get to a meeting in 1313."

The doorman smirked, "Well, there ain't no 1313. There's no 13th floor in this building. You sure you have the right place?"

I looked at Gloria and summoned her intervention. She took the cue, "Okay buddy, we've been coming here for the last two weeks for meetings with a guy we were supposed to interview. He didn't show up tonight and we want to check on him."

The doorman thumbed through the pages of the visitor log, "You say you've been a visitor every day for two weeks. Can you remember what time of day you arrived?"

I explained, "We would meet him every morning at 8 a.m."

The door man went back ten pages and looked at each page, "So, it was Mister what?"

"Bronck, Jonas Bronck."

The doorman looked up, "Hey, I'm sorry, but there's not one entry for Bronck. You sure you have the right building? This is the Qenatas Arms."

Gloria stepped closer to the desk, "Look at the key, man. Can we at least see the elevator?"

With a real New Yorker attitude, "Sure be my guest, but you can't go up. You got that?"

Gloria smiled, "Sure, no problem."

We moved quickly to the elevator. We called it to the ground floor and when it opened we stepped in. It was a different, newer elevator than what we had been using. Our eyes quickly found the button panel. There was no 13th floor.

Gloria wanted to go pound on the all the doors of the 12th and 14th floors. She suggested we see if the key worked in 1213 or 1413, but I stopped her.

I looked down at her, "Gloria this has all been an illusion. For some reason Ida wanted to have one final little joke. She got what she wanted; a full week of programming about God on a major network. Who knew she was so religious."

Gloria and I walked past the doorman and she had to joke, "You were right, wrong building. We were looking for the Gotcha Arms on Avenue F."

The doorman shook his head then added, "Hey, you guys know there ain't no Avenue F, right? And by the way, I called my boss and he said in the old days there used to be a 13th floor, but it was taken out ten years ago, you know bad luck?"

As we got out onto the street, I handed her the key and walked her to the corner. I hugged her and told her that we should probably not mention this God experience ever again.

She smiled and said, "Hey, it was an amazing journey. You can write a book about it someday. Why don't we share a cab? You look like you could use a friend."

I patted her on the shoulder and told her, "No, I want to walk a bit and think this all out."

She got into the taxi and as it pulled away she smiled from the window and waved goodbye.

As I walked across town to Washington Square, I thought about my mother and my father. What would they have thought about what happened tonight? Would they have been proud of me? Would they think that questioning God would help or hurt my chances of getting into heaven? I don't know who that faceless force was in that room. Was it just a clever prankster or some hallucination? I started to think about my career in TV. Was it over?

56.   Epilogue

I finally did get in a cab that night and headed home. We passed the national debt sign ticking away forever and then passed the Apple store and all the other places that represent civilization today. I looked at the ads for all the things that were supposed to make life better. I wondered what God would think about 4G.

I thought about being one of those 20,000 people on the Earth one million years ago. What would I believe? I could see the sun move, but the Earth beneath my feet did not. How could I possibly know that I was moving 1,000 miles an hour? I can only believe what I can see and one thing was for sure, at this point in my life I haven't seen God.

In the TV business nothing stays the same. People move, networks revamp, management pushes for higher ratings. It's not a glacier, it's a bulldozer. With the death of Steve Summerville ruled an accident I couldn't help but think that the "accident" was just, Steve being Steve, making decisions in his own timeframe. We will never know.

As far as TNN was concerned, the new guy came in and decided that he had to put his mark on the place like a dog marking his territory. A lot of good people were thrown by the wayside to make way for the new visionary's progressive news network. They replaced my show with documentaries they bought on the cheap and packed with dozens of commercials.

I decided to travel the world and find truth. Lofty goal, yes, but I had to get out of the rat race. With my notebook and a small camera I began another journey to all points of the Earth. I had always been a big fan of W. Somerset Maugham and his book *The Razor's Edge* with its epigraph, "the wise say the path to salvation is hard." I didn't think I was looking for salvation, but knew that as long as kept moving I could delay any damnation that was coming my way.

What prompted my desire to travel was something that happened shortly after my contract wasn't renewed at TNN. I was walking near Times Square after lunch and as I turned the corner, I was facing the subway steps of an uptown station and there she was; Ida Pearlstein. I ran as fast I could without being run down in traffic. I screamed, "Ida, Ida, please wait!"

I got to the station and entered. The platform was packed with midday travelers. I walked from one end of the platform to the other checking every face. I am sure people thought I was just another crazy person in the New York subway. I did not find her or anyone who looked like her.

Since that day, I've seen someone looking like her dressed in her black and white suit with a black and white hat in Singapore, Paris, Dubai and Mumbai. I thought I was going mad. I thought maybe this could have been the same thing that the followers of Jesus experienced after his death?

In my state of mind I had this strong desire to ask one more question. I wanted one more lunch or have that one last conversation. I was curious about why she did what she did and how did she pulled it off.

A wise man in Tibet told me, "Just talk to her each night before you go to bed and you will stop seeing her. She just wants to be in your life."

I got it. It was just like praying to God right before you go to bed; a primitive desire to survive the night.

As for Gloria, she moved on to another network and I'm happy to report she is on the air as a talk show host. Every couple of months, no matter where I am in the world I get a text that simply says: I love you, I miss you. And that is all a guy can ask for from my wunderkind. Gloria gets good ratings because she prepares and has no fear. She is a good person and a great journalist. They used to say that I was the boy wonder, but now I am an older wiser man who has no desire to be in front of the camera. I just want to find something that cannot be taught in a studio or in a university.

As I look at the wonders of the world I think how many people must have lost their lives building those pyramids by moving twenty-five ton blocks of stone. And how many more people will lose their lives in the world fighting over land or for their brand of religion or simply drawing a cartoon in an attempt to show someone another point of view. The experience of "A Week with God" showed me some things about myself. I am never going to learn the whole truth. There are no absolutes.

Mankind has always been a little closed-minded. But some brave souls became curious and set out to find out what was over the hill. Imagine what the world would be like today if Columbus or the Vikings had not ventured out of their villages. Unfortunately, many times, the purpose of their venturing was to conquer and force their customs and beliefs on others. We still persecute those who may not think the way we do.

When we developed a language we told stories. Even with the written word, we had a hazy grasp of time. We will never truly understand what happened in our past. Humans have trouble remembering details of a few days ago, let alone decades. Think about how many years have passed since man started to walk upright. Some say the answer is 240,000 years, while our Earth, in its present state, has been around for about 4.54 billion years. The world changed. People have changed. How many more decades do we have on our blue planet?

Even if we could travel at the speed of light, it would take hundreds of thousands of years to get to the edge of the Milky Way and back. Your family would be gone. Maybe even your planet would be gone. Remember a light-year is the distance that light can travel in one year. Turn off all the lights in a room and turn on a flashlight. See if you can determine how fast the light travels to the wall. Now imagine how far that light would travel in a year. Our minds are inadequate.

Time is so vast we cannot do the calculation of how long it took God to create Earth. Sure the Bible says it was six days and then he rested, but in reality the big bang or the beginning of the universe took place 13.7 billion years ago. It took 9 billion years to create the Earth and then more than 13 billion years to create life on the planet. Using some rough math here that would mean that, if the Bible is correct, each day was really two billion years. And using the biblical scripture as a guide, God rested on the seventh day. That means God is still in his 2 billion year rest. Perhaps that is why he didn't make it to the studio that night.

Your life and my life are really small little microscopic dots on the timeline of the planet Earth. Think about all the good people and children who have been taken so early in their lives. How does God justify this? Certainly if you believe in a loving God you must be brave enough to ask the question: why would God treat the very finest human beings with such disregard?

For many people the reason we must have a supreme being in our lives is fear. We fear time most of all. We feel dwarfed by the vastness of the universe, and we should. If our primal wiring was meant to do anything it was to help us survive and to populate the planet. We're generation makers with a firm commitment to our longevity. Fear of the unknown has always been there. No matter what we invent and no matter how far we travel we will always have the curiosity and fear and excitement of knowing what lies beyond the boundary.

We can theorize how things work, but until we hold it in our hands and see it with our own two eyes we are suspicious. We're like a young child imagining that the shadows on the dark bedroom wall are ghosts coming to take us away. Our biggest fear is what happens to our essence, our soul and our minds after we die. This mounting fear bubbles below the surface of our consciousness from the first moment we encounter death.

When fear becomes a deterrent to logical thought, mankind's evolution from animal to highly evolved species is thwarted. There is a difference between believing and knowing. If you blindly follow a belief without any desire to know more, then you may find it difficult to respect others who do not view the world as you do. How can anyone know what God really wants?

It took man so long to get to this point and it will take many centuries to find a way to deal with the fear of death and a need for a God-based compass. Death isn't going down a tunnel of bright lights and reunions with dead relatives. Death is when you get to go back into the Earth and be part of the ever expanding universe. This is not your choice and everyone will die.

To think that less than 100 years ago many people carried a dead rabbit's foot in their pocket to bring them good luck. They believed that the talisman would keep them from evil spirits along the way. Not so great for the rabbit, but this was something people believed without any proof at all.

As I see the wonders of the world and think about my friend Ida Pearlstein and what she did for me, I am at peace knowing that she changed my life. I haven't seen her in a while, but perhaps I'll see her again. That love and need just might be one of the forces behind the reason we need God. We want to believe in an afterlife so we can see those people we love just one more time.

This journey for truth must continue. You may come to your own conclusions, but whether you're a homeless person or a King or Queen, you will die. That makes us all commoners in the eyes of God. How man permits the elevation of certain DNA to the level of royalty has never made any sense to me. Many things men and women have done in the last 2.4 million years would disgrace even the devil.

For me the journey is never over until I can no longer write a sentence that means something to another person. Until then I will continue my quest. For those just starting out on the voyage, there is some good news up ahead. The more you know, the less fear you have. Each year, I am less and less afraid.

Books that influenced this work

1984 by George Orwell - Published: June 8, 1949

Holy Bible (King James Version) by various writers – Published 1611

The God Delusion by Richard Dawkins – Published in 2006

The Case for Christ by Lee Stobel – Published in 1998

god is not great by Christopher Hitchens – Published in 2008

Muhammad by Sarah Conover – Published in 2013

The Grand Design by Stephen Hawking - Published in 2010

A History of God by Karen Armstrong – Published in 1993

The Future of the Mind by Michio Kaku – Published in 2014

The Believing Brain by Michael Shermer – Published in 2011

Debating Christian Theism by J.P Morland, Chad Meister, Khaldoun A. Sweis - Published in 2013

GOD - The Failed Hypothesis by Victor J. Stenger – Published in 2007

Thank you very much

Ideas for books are illusive and difficult. What started out to be a conversation about God turned into an idea for this story. At a lunch with my good friend Andrew Economos, I described the plot of the book. He looked up from his salad and said, "Write it." Thank you.

At the same time, I was helping some friends with some nasty computer problems and had the opportunity to have several dinners with Audrey and Seymour Topping, well known writers, who helped me walk around the holes in the story. They also nourished my desire to write this book and bring it to fruition. I thank them for permitting me to repair their computers and inspiring me to write.

Next, a writer needs a place to write. My significant other, Roxy Myzal, was motivational in so many ways. She was gracious in letting me use her Adirondack cabin after I sent her back to the city. I will always remember her words of encouragement, "You are using up our vacation by writing! This better be a good book."

There are people who we loving refer to as 'readers' and they get to see the ugly duckling before it grows up. To them, I owe a great amount of gratitude. Judith Economos first sliced and diced the work and made it readable. Mike

Powell, my friend and authentic British speaker, was able to get my style and format into something that mirrored the professional look of publishing.

To my oldest friend and college chum, Kenny Lee, I give a warm amount of sympathy for sitting through hundreds of lunches where I would bounce ideas off him. His reinforcement of the good ideas and jokes helped me understand how to keep a story moving. As they say, timing is everything. And to Diana Stokey thank you for your notes and encouragement as well.

To Aimee Lim for her fantastic cover design and Jim Valle for his photographic efforts on the project, thank you so much for your creativity and talent.

And finally, to my mother Mary Elizabeth Douglas, who left this world at the age of 92 as I began to write this book, I must thank her for everything. It was her support when I was an elementary student that made be believe that I was a writer. Even when I knew nothing about writing, she told me I could. So I did.

About the Author

Dwight C. Douglas was born in Pittsburgh, PA and started working at the age of ten as a Pittsburgh Press newspaper delivery person. Having the opportunity to read the newspaper everyday fueled his desire to read and write. After winning several writing contests in elementary and high school, he went on to attend Point Park University and studied Journalism and Communication.

During college, he worked on the PBS TV show *Mister Rogers Neighborhood* as a film-telecine technician. At the age of twenty he left college to work for ABC radio as they were developing their FM properties. After working at several radio stations in Pittsburgh and Washington, DC,

Douglas moved to Atlanta to join the largest radio consulting firm in the world, Burkhart-Abrams & Associates, where he later became president and worked with media companies around the world. During that 25 year period, he was instrumental in recruiting and coaching high-profile morning shows, including Howard Stern.

He moved to New York in 2000 to be the vice president of marketing for a worldwide software company. He also produces a comedy web site. Throughout his career he has written screenplays, books and magazine articles. For more information see www.thedreamwindow.com